Anna Wilson has two black cats called Ink and Jet. She was always a Cat–Type Person until she got her gorgeous black Labrador, Kenna. Now she is a Cat-AND-Dog-Type Person, and she keeps chickens and a tortoise too. She has just about enough space in her house for her husband and two children as well. They all live together in Bradford on Avon in Wiltshire. Anna has written many young-fiction titles for Macmillan Children's Books and plans to write many, many more!

Puppy Power

TOP of the PUPS

Anna Wilson

Illustrated by Moira Munro

MACMILLAN CHILDREN'S BOOKS

First published 2009 by Macmillan Children's Books

This edition published 2015 by Macmillan Children's Books
an imprint of Pan Macmillan
a division of Macmillan Publishers Limited
20 New Wharf Road, London N1 9RR
Associated companies throughout the world
www.panmacmillan.com

ISBN 978-1-4472-7613-5

Text copyright © Anna Wilson 2009
Illustrations copyright © Moira Munro 2009

The right of Anna Wilson and Moira Munro to be identified as the
author and illustrator of this work has been asserted by them in
accordance with the Copyright, Designs and Patents Act 1988.

1 3 5 7 9 8 6 4 2

A CIP catalogue record for this book is available from
the British Library.

Typeset by Nigel Hazle
Printed and bound by CPI Group (UK) Ltd, Croydon CR0 4YY

For my cousin Liz, with thanks for
all the Breeding Information

Contents

1
How to Get Nostalgic

Quite a lot of time has gone
by since I last felt the
need to write about me and
my Perfect Pooch, Honey.
Since becoming TRULY
BONDED AS A pAIR
through learning some mega-
faberoony training tricks last summer,
Honey and I had been getting along like a
House on Fire, which means that we were even
more the best of friends than we were *before* she
learned how to behave beautifully.

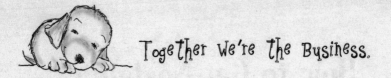

Together We're the Business.

I have to say, it was becoming a Pup Idol that did it, in my opinion. After winning a prize for some totally fantabulous dancing, Honey's brain seemed to suddenly click into understanding that if she did what I asked, life would be much better for All Concerned.

In other words, *if* she stopped eating all the food in the fridge and my sister April's flip-flops, not to mention her mobile phone and other personal ACCESSORIES, and *if* she stopped jumping up and running in crazy circles and generally behaving like a totally doolally nightmare, everyone would love her more.

Even me.

And I pretty much loved her one hundred and ten per cent to start with.

Who wouldn't love a cute pooch like me?

In fact, over all, Honey had really calmed down these days. Even April had stopped calling her 'that mutt', and she actually sometimes stopped and stroked Honey or gave her a pat on the head. In fact, she even *volunteered* to walk Honey sometimes after work with her boyfriend, Nick (who was also Honey's vet).

It had all become quite nice and easy.

'Do you know, Summer,' Mum said, 'I never thought I would say this, but Honey is so quiet these days that sometimes I almost forget she's there.'

Hmmm.

When Mum said this, I felt quite a NOSTALGIC kind of feeling that sprang out of nowhere. This is a word my Bestest Friend Molly told me, which means that you realize that things that happened in the past were really rather nice, in other words you have a YEARNING for the way they were before.

Honey had been such a cute little pupsicle, and now she was a big dog who was loving and adorable, but maybe just a teensy bit not as fun . . .

Fun? I'm fun! I like fun! Look!

In fact, the more I thought it over and pondered, the more I realized this: the actual Truth of the Matter was . . .

Life as a dog owner had got a bit pREDICTABLE.

I suppose my feelings of predictableness were not helped by the fact that I was by then in Year Five, which was quite a grown-up

and serious place to be in the General Order
of School Life. It seemed that the moment you
went into Year Five, teachers decided you
had to be given twice as much homework
as a normal human being can reasonably be
expected to cope with. I mean, I knew I was
going to be in Double Figures in the summer
term, in other words I would be ten, which
is quite nice, as it meant April wouldn't be
able to get away with calling me her 'Baby
Sister' any more. But why did this mean that
I had to know the names of all the rivers in
the United Kingdom and the dates that all the
various Invaders decided to come and have
boring battles all over the place? What earthly
use was any of that information to the average
ten-year-old? It would have been much more
practical to my day-to-day life in the Real
World if our teacher, Mrs Wotherspoon, would
tell us how to get the most from the extremely

MINUSCULE amount of pocket money that I received, or how to learn all the words to the *High Street Musical* songs so that I could audition to go on my favourite telly programme, *Seeing Stars,* and wouldn't have to RELY on tiny amounts of pocket money in the first place.

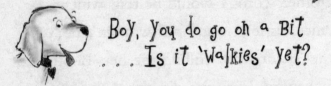

Boy, You do go on a Bit
... Is it 'Walkies' yet?

All this homework did not leave much time for SOCIALIZING – in other words, hanging out with Molly, or anyone else for that matter. Life was too serious.

I was thinking about this after a particularly yawnsome day at school when Mum came home and said, 'Get your coat. We've got to take Honey for her annual check-up, remember?'

How to Get Nostalgic

I had forgotten about this. Honey needed to have injections and a check-up with the vet once a year to make sure that her teeth were all right and that she didn't have fleas and that her General Health and Well-Being was, er, generally healthy and well-beingish.

When we arrived, there was a Din and Clamouring of a commotion coming from inside the waiting room that was worse than usual.

Mum caught my eye as we walked in through the door and said, 'What a racket!'

'Yes,' I agreed. 'Anyone would think that a plague of catastrophic proportions has flooded the region and made all the animals in the district as Sick As Parrots.'

Ouch, my ears hurt.

As it turned out, there really was a parrot in the waiting room! If he had been an actual sick

7

sick parrot, I would have eaten my duffle coat
there and then, because he
seemed anything *but* ill. He was
certainly making more of a
Rumpus than a normally
sick person or animal
would do. He was talking
very loudly, saying quite rude things
about the people in the waiting room.

'Look at the ears on that!' he said, and I am
sure he pointed his beak in the exact direction
of a man with such huge ears you might think
he was the BFG or something.

Normally I would have found this all
highly hilarious. But I was not in a mood of
Hilarity. I was in a mood of utter Dullness.

So was Honey.

Another day, another parrot
squawking.

How to Get Nostalgic

'Honey,' I said to her, as she lay on the floor waiting patiently, 'if you think sitting in the vets' waiting room is boring, you should think yourself lucky you are not a girl in Year Five who has to add fractions and remember who Beowulf is.'

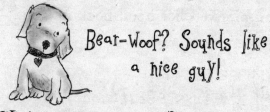

Bear-Woof? Sounds like a nice guy!

'Who's got a big nose then?' yelled the parrot, pointing his beak this time at someone who looked like a clown on his day off who had forgotten to remove part of his outfit.

'Don't fancy yours much!' he squawked at a man who was sitting with a lady who was not the prettiest of feminine types, even if you were trying hard to be kind and think of something nice to say.

Just as the man with big ears looked as

though he was going to pick up the parrot's cage and fling it against the wall of the waiting area, another man walked in and everyone, even the big-eared man, turned to look and said, 'Ahhhhh!'

Honey looked up in a mildly interested manner, then plonked her head back on the floor again.

What's all the fuss about?

 The man had the tiniest, squidgiest, softest-looking bundle in his arms.

'Look, Mum! Look!' I hissed. But Mum was already looking, and the expression on her face was one that I had not seen since . . . well, since

Honey had been a tiny, squidgy, soft-looking bundle.

'It's a puppy!' Mum squeaked, rather unnecessarily, as we could all see that.

Hey! I'm Better looking than that little guy . . .

'Oh, Mum – do you remember when Honey looked like that?' I whispered.

Mum nodded. Then she sighed. 'It makes me feel quite emotional,' she said.

'Why's that?' I asked, carefully keeping my voice low. I hoped she wasn't going to actually *get* all Emotional right there in a Public Place. On the scale of Mortifyingly Embarrassing Parental Moments, that would probably score at least one million.

It didn't matter though. Everyone in the room was cooing over the puppy and the parrot was shrieking, 'Hello! Hello! Look at me!' at the top of its squawky voice.

'Well, Honey's a big girl now. You're ten – TEN! I can hardly believe it. And as for April . . . I hardly see her these days, what with her job at the solicitors and all the time she spends with Nick. All my girls are growing up.'

I did feel a bit sorry for Mum. She looked really quite sad. I put my arm around her and we both sat staring at the tiny puppy.

Then Honey sat up and licked Mum's hand. It was like she was hugging Mum too.

I'm still your Number One Fan!

And that is when I had my totally inspirationalist idea.

'Hey, Mum – *why don't we get another puppy?*' I asked.

Mum turned to look at me, her eyes wide

and shiny, and I felt very proud of myself
for coming up so mega-speedily with such a
Stunningly Intelligent and Thoughtful Solution
to Mum's emotionalism.

'A new puppy?' she said. 'I don't think so,
Summer Holly Love.'

2

How to Come up with an Alternative Option

I was completely flabbergasted with Mum's totally Underwhelming Reaction to my brilliant brainflash of an idea. My mouth hung open in amazement, but I didn't have time to think of a Suitable Response, because Nick came out at that moment and called us in for Honey's appointment.

We followed him into his Consulting Room, which is where the vet Consults with the animals to see what is wrong with them. (Although how an actual human can talk with an actual animal is beyond me, unless he has

14

developed the magical powers of someone who can understand animal languages like people in films and stories.)

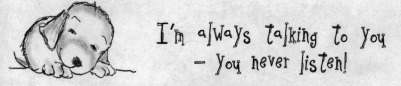

I'm always talking to you – You never listen!

As we went in I muttered to Mum, 'I don't see what is such a terrible idea about having another dog.'

Mum hissed, 'Not now, Summer.'

'What's up?' Nick asked. 'Did I just hear you say something about getting another dog?'

'No, nothing like that,' said Mum, doing the fake smiley face she does to other grown-ups to cover up the fact that she's annoyed.

'We haven't discussed it properly yet,' I said, giving Mum a GLARY STARE.

Nick smiled. 'Oh, I see.' He looked at

15

Honey and ruffled her head. 'One's enough when it's as beautiful as this little girl, isn't it?'

Honey closed her eyes and snuggled into Nick.

 This guy gives good cuddles.

Mum nodded most vigorously. 'Absolutely. I mean, I know Honey can get a bit lonely sometimes when we're out, but I just can't

How to Come up with an Alternative Option

face going through all that house training and the chewing and the accidents on the carpet for a second time . . .'

I sighed heavily.

Nick looked at me. 'Your mum's right, you know, Summer. Having two dogs is an even bigger responsibility than one. You know: double the mess, double the vets' bills—'

'OK!' I butted in (a bit rudely, I know, but what was Nick doing, putting Mum off like this?). 'But we've just seen the most gorgeous puppy in the waiting room and it made me so nostalgical, and even Mum said she was sad that her girls were growing up and not around so much, especially April because she's been spending all her extra time with you—'

'Summer!' Mum almost growled at me, and looked a bit red in the face.

What had I said now?

Nick looked as if he'd gone a bit red too,

17

for some bizarre reason. He bent down to stroke Honey. What was wrong in Grown-Upsville today? I thought in a bewildered fashion. They were obviously doing that thing where they can communicate on a different length of wave from younger people who are, as I had always known, much more normal than they are. So I ignored the red faces and said, 'So shall we get on with the vaccinationing then?'

'Sure,' said Nick. 'I'm just waiting for the nurse. So it's a check-up today? There's nothing specific I need to look out for?'

'No, Honey's doing really well – very healthy,' I said proudly.

'She certainly is a beautiful Lab,' Nick said as he got up and went to get the vaccination medicine out of a white cupboard on the wall. 'You know what? Maybe you should think about breeding from her. If you don't want

to get another dog, but you're missing those early puppy days, it could be a lot of fun for everyone. Have you kept all the pedigree paperwork from when you first got her?'

As he spoke a wave of rushing excitement was whooshing up from my heart to my head. 'Wooo!' I cried, jumping up and down and clapping my hands. 'Puppies! What a fantastical idea!' I flung my arms around Honey. 'Who's the mummy, Honey?'

No idea!

I looked at Mum with my cutest pleading expression and said, 'Pur-leeeese, Mum? Can Honey have puppies?'

Mum was frowning and chewing her lip. 'Hmmm,' she said.

Nick looked as if he realized he had just put his foot in something unfortunate and

19

he started babbling. 'Listen, I didn't mean to stir up trouble, Angela,' he said to my mum (because that is her actual name, and he can't exactly call her Mrs Love when he is a fully grown-up person and so is she). 'It just suddenly occurred to me that we haven't had a conversation about Honey's fertility recently, and we probably should, because if you don't want to breed from her you really should get her spayed while she's still young.'

I was standing in between them, feeling a bit OVERWHELMED WITH BAFFLEMENT at all the medical-ish type words that Nick was using. I made a mental reminder to look them all up in my book *Love Me, Love My Dog*, which is about all things dog-related and is very informative for when you don't know something about your pooch. Nick was babbling really quite fast now, using lots of difficult words, and Mum's face was

How to Come up with an Alternative Option

going from frowning not-suredness through to shockedness and puzzledness. My hands started going a bit damp from nerves.

Just as I thought Mum might say, 'I'm beginning to wish I had not said yes to having a dog at all!' or something equally distressing, the door to the Consulting Room opened.

Love Me, Love My Dog

Monica Sitstill

'Hello, Nick. Do you need me now? Heeheeheehee!'

'Yes, er, thank you, Felicity,' Nick said, his face going even redder than before. 'Angela, Summer, this is our new veterinary nurse – Felicity Shufflebottom.'

SHUFFLEBOTTOM? SHUFFLE followed by BOTTOM? *All in the same name?* Was there really a name of such comedical proportions? It made being called Summer Love seem positively boring and run-off-the-hill in its normality. No wonder Nick was red in the face!

The Bottom Shuffler giggled in a way that reminded me of April. I suppose she was embarrassed about her name. She tossed her head around like April too, and I noticed that her blonde hair was tied back in a long swishy ponytail. This was probably to stop it getting covered in blood and medicine and stuff while she was working.

'Are you ready to do the vaccinations, Nick?' she asked, blinking a lot as if she had something in her eye.

Nick muttered, 'Yes, Felicity. Would you please hold on to Honey here and distract her while I inject her?'

Honestly, I thought, is that all

How to Come up with an Alternative Option

she's here for? I could have done that. You don't exactly need a Universal Degree in Veterinary-Type Nursing to give a dog a few cuddles.

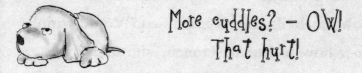

More cuddles? – OW!
That hurt!

Nick was as careful as always when he stuck the needle in, but Honey still felt it and she tried to whip round and nip him. However, the Bottom Shuffler obviously had a Grip of Iron, because Honey could not get free. (Maybe you do need a Universal Degree after all, so that you can disguise your Grip of Iron into a normal cuddle-type situation.)

I was glad that I had got over my unfortunate habit of fainting whenever I saw needles, as I would not have wanted the Bottom Shuffler to try to catch *me* with her Grip of Iron. I was getting a distinctively

23

strong whiff of her perfume, which was in the Category of overwhelmingness and not a perfume I wanted to get any closer to, thank you very much.

Mum looked very impressed. 'You certainly know how to handle Honey,' she said to the Bottom Shuffler.

'Oh, it's all down to having such a good teacher,' she replied, and blinked hard at Nick again.

I wondered if I should offer her a hanky or get some water to help her sort out her eyes. They were quite obviously causing her a lot of botheration.

'Yes, well, thank you, Felicity,' said Nick. 'You can go now.'

'She's quite a character,' said Mum, smirking, as the nurse shuffled her bottom out of the room.

'Hmm,' said Nick, raising his eyebrows.

24

How to Come up with an Alternative Option

Then he changed the subject (thank the high heavens, as it was hardly a very interesting one) and went back to talking about my pooch. 'Well, that's Honey done for today. I've noted everything in her health record book. And, er, do have a bit of a think about what you want to do with her as regards breeding, won't you, Angela? I don't know if it would make any difference, but I would be keen to help out if you did decide to . . .' He trailed off.

Mum was frowning again. 'Thank you, Nick. We'll think about it.'

I didn't like the sound of that last bit. It was what Mum said when she was actually saying something quite different inside her own head.

In other words, a Big Fat **NO**.

Can we go now?

3

How to Nearly Get Someone on Your Wavelength

Once we got home Honey bounded out into the garden to chase leaves. I didn't blame her. I would have done too, if I'd had a morning of being poked by needles while being held in a Grip of Iron.

Home, sweet home!

Mum put the kettle on and then she fixed me with a very serious face and said, 'Summer, I think we need to talk about this puppy idea.'

How to Nearly Get Someone on Your Wavelength

'Faberoony—' I started.

But Mum held up a hand and shook her head. 'No, Summer, what I was going to say was, please don't get your hopes up.'

April came in at that moment, which was probably a good thing as it stopped me from stamping my foot and putting on a very SCoWLY face, which is what I felt like doing, but which is never a particularly Effective Way of getting Mum to come round to my way of thinking, I have found.

'You two look serious. What's up?' April asked.

Normally I would have been severely irritated by my sister sticking her pointy nose into a Private Conversation, but this time I was actually quite relieved. Perhaps April would be able to De-Fuse the Tension of the situation.

'*Nick* says we should think about letting Honey have puppies, and *Mum* says I must not

27

hope for that happening at all EVER,' I said, trying to put the emphasis on it being *Nick's* idea, and also trying to put the emphasis on *Mum's* meanness.

'I didn't say that,' Mum cut in.

April is never normally on my side of anything, but she *does* think, in a most cringesome manner, that *everything* Nick says and does is pRACTICALLY pERFECT IN EvERY WAY, as Mary Poppins would say.

And for once things went According to Plan.

'I think Nick's got a point, Mum,' said April. 'I mean, he must know what he's talking about. He *is* a vet.'

Mum raised her eyebrows. 'No! Really?' she said, in a sarcastical manner, which was not at all mumlike, in my opinion.

April frowned. 'Mum,' she said in her I'm-trying-oh-so-hard-to-be-patient-with-you-but-you-do-make-it-difficult voice, 'tell me what Nick *actually* said. Did he say it would be good for Honey to have puppies?'

Mum took a deep INHALATION, which means that she breathed in very noisily. And then she huffed moodily. 'Now why do I get the feeling I am being ganged up on here?' she said, tightly crossing her arms. I couldn't help noticing, however, that there was a tiny bit of a smile flickering away in the corner of her mouth.

'The thing is, Mum,' April continued, as if she had also spotted the tiny bit of a smile and thought it might be worth Persevering, 'Nick and I have really enjoyed walking Honey recently, and we thought, you know, if we got our own dog—'

'What's all this "we"?' Mum asked. The tiny bit of a smile had disappeared rather quickly.

April blushed. 'Well, we were thinking of getting a place together,' she said quietly.

'Oh,' Mum said.

Yippee! I thought. April's going to move out! Hurrah! No more bathroom lock-ins so that no one else can get to the loo or the shower when they want it. No more face-pack gunkitis in the fridge! No more shrieking and hair flicking all about the place!

'Nick didn't mention anything about you

two moving in together when we saw him this morning,' said Mum.

April sagged her shoulders and flopped her head back and rolled her eyes, which is her way of saying 'DERRRRRR!'

'MUM!' she said. 'As if Nick would talk to *you* about *our* private life!'

I thought I ought to step in and try to De-Fuse this new bit of Tension, as April was not actually helping the Let's Talk About Puppies plan. 'Anyway,' I said, 'we saw Nick in a Professional Capacity today, so he wouldn't have wanted to talk about personal things, especially in front of his new nurse—'

'*New nurse?*' April said, in a sharp tone of speaking. 'What new nurse?' Mum shot me a Glance that seemed to involve a lot of eyebrow wiggling. It made her look somewhat Demented. 'Nick never said anything about a new nurse. Is she pretty? What's her name?'

31

'Yes,' I carried on, ignoring Mum's weird flickering facial movements. 'She is kind of pretty in a long-blonde-hair sort of way – bit like you, actually – but get this: she's got the looniest name you have ever heard of in the history of all things loony! She's called Felicity Shufflebottom!'

'I don't care if she's called Mavis Bumwiggle!' April shouted. 'Nick didn't tell me he had a new nurse who is PRETTY!'

And she's got a Grip of Iron.

At the sound of the shouting Honey zoomed into the kitchen and jumped around crazily at April's feet. But April was Not In The Mood. In fact, she was suddenly in a Very Bad Mood indeed. She turned on her high heels and swooshed out of the room, leaving me with my mouth hanging open and Mum staring at me

and shaking her head like I had just said the most insulting thing known to the human race. Whatever that might be.

'Well done, Summer,' said Mum. 'You really know how to put your foot in it, don't you?'

'Why? What have I done?' I cried in a protesting fashion. April is always spinning on her heels so fast you could probably plug her into a socket and make electricity from her. (It might solve all the world's Global Greenhouse Problems actually, now I come to think of it.) Why should it suddenly be my fault that she had spun off in a huff *this* time?

Mum sighed. 'You will find out only too soon that love is a complicated and many splendoured thing,' she said dramatically.

If Molly had been there, I would have rolled my eyes at her from under my fringe and curled my top lip to show her that I was not

33

responsible in any way for my mum's
FLIp-DI-DOO-DAH nonsense way of
talking. 'Mum,' I said, 'I'm going to call
Molly, OK?'

Mum nodded and looked sadly at Honey,
who was still whizzing around in circles in a
random and slightly annoying fashion.

Welcome to the House of Extreme
Looniness, I thought. I had to get
out of there. Fast.

Take me With you!

4
How to Get Puppy Power

Phew! Molly answered the phone, which meant I did not have to have a polite yet time-wasting conversation with her mum or dad along the lines of, 'Hello, Mrs/Mr Cook (delete as appropriate). How are you? Really? I'm so glad. Fine. Thank you. Yes, it is warm for the time of year . . . blah-di-blah-di-blah-di-blah . . .'

'Hey, Molls!' I shouted.

'Summer!' she shouted back. 'I'm so glad you've called. You'll never guess what I've just got!'

'You'll never believe it, but Nick says

35

Honey should possibly definitely maybe have pup—'

I was forced to stop suddenly in mid-tracks. Molly was actually screaming at me down the phone and sounded even more excited than I was. Surely she was not getting a puppy or a dog that could have puppies or—

I had to pull the phone away from my ear because the level of shrieking was in danger of bursting my ear's drum, which I have heard is a very dangerous thing indeed if it happens, because you could end up with only one ear working, which would be very UNSETTLING as it could make you lose your balance and feel wobbly – in other words, FREAKSOME.

With the phone away from my ear in this manner, Molly's voice was so distant and high pitched that it sounded like those voices in cartoons when someone is babbling on the

36

other end of the phone and you can't quite hear what they are saying. Molly in a cartoon would be a fab idea, I thought, as she squeaked away. How would she be drawn, I wondered? Maybe she would look like that character with the vastly tall hairstyle that is blue?

'Summer! Summer?'

I put the phone back to my ear.

'Yes?' I said.

'Oh, I thought we'd been cut off for a moment,' said Molly. 'So, what do you think?'

'I can't wait!' I said, thinking Molly was asking me what I thought about Honey possibly becoming a mum.

'Can't wait for what?' said Molly in a puzzled tone.

'For Honey to have puppies,' I said, also in a puzzled tone. Had she not listened to what I said?

'HONEY HAVING PUPPIES?! OH HOW

37

FABEROONY!' she
shrieked again.

'MOLLY,' I
shrieked back,
'PLEASE STOP
SHRIEKING! YOU
ARE SEVERELY
WOUNDING THE
DRUMS IN MY EARS!'

'Sorry,' she said in her normal voice.
'But it's just such mega-fantastic news! And
now that I have Puppy Power, we can get all
kinds of information from that which will be
astonishingly useful for the puppies.'

'Right,' I said, realizing that *I* had not in
fact been listening to *Molly* properly because of
all the shrieking, and I had not one iota of an
idea of what Puppy Power actually was.

'I'm coming right over!' said Molly. 'Do
NOT move, under any circumstances.'

38

How to Get Puppy Power

★

I didn't have time to move far as Molly was at the door literally four minutes and thirty-four seconds later. She was jumping up and down, which is what she does when she is OVER THE TOP OF THE MOON with excitability.

'Look what I got from my auntie as a late birthday present!' she yelled.

All I could see was a little pink thing in her hand that looked rather like an oblong wallet or box.

Not another totally yawnsome addition to my already overflowingly BORING life, I thought . . .

I told Molly to come in, as she was starting to create quite a palaver of a spectacle and it was risking being totally attention-making if a neighbour or someone from school saw her. Rosie Chubb was the person I was most thinking of. Rosie thought we had all become the bestest mates after the Talent Contest, when Molly and I had saved her from one hundred and million per cent social death on the dance floor. But since then she had seemed dead set on having Molly for herself – in other words, making sure I was well and truly Out of the Picture. But it was bad luck for her because she did not Get the Message that Molly and I were a DYNAMIC DUo, and *we* had learned pretty quickly that there was no way we wanted our Duo to become a Trio. So we were always trying to avoid Rosie Chubb.

'You have got to see this!' Molly was still shrieking. She whizzed ahead of me into the room which Mum still calls the playroom even though I stopped Playing in it about a hundred years ago (I call it the Den – *much* more sophisticateder), slammed the door and bounded

on to a beanbag with the pink thing in her hand. She opened it up like it was a little treasure box, and that's when I realized what it was — a GameGirl!

'Oh my giddy aunts!' I said in an EXCLAMATORY manner, completely forgetting that I had wanted to talk to Molly about Honey becoming a mum.

You had COMPLETELY forgotten aBout me, in fact.

'Exactly!' shrieked Molly. 'She is a pretty dudey giddy aunt too.' ('Dudey' is Molly's newest word. Apparently it means something is mega-faberoony.) 'And yes, this is indeed what I think you think this is — a GAMEGIRL!' I was going to have to tell her to Put A Lid on it if she did not stop the shrieking thing. 'But not only that, the game on it is . . .' She tapped

41

the screen, and suddenly I knew what all the shrieking excitability was about.

'PUPPY POWER!' we yelled together.

I had finally got on to the length of wave that Molly was on. And what a huge smasher of a wave it was. 'You are *so* lucky!' I cried. 'Let's have a look.'

Mum does not 'believe in' computer games, so I'm not allowed one. I've always thought this is daft of her, as they obviously do exist so how can she not believe in them? They aren't like fairies or dragons, for instance.

Molly opened the pink box, which had controls on one side and a screen on the other. As she turned it on and waited for it to sort of wake up, like all computerified things have to do, I thought about how, no matter how many faberoony presents she got, Molly always moaned about her birthday because it was right at the beginning of September when school had not started yet. This meant no one could ever come to her party. Except me, of course. That year we had gone out with Molly's mum and dad, which Molly said was totally un-cool and in no way dudey.

I had personally thought it was an Outstandingly Good Deal in the way of a birthday treat as we had gone to the cinema and had a pizza, *and* Molly's parents had sat a million miles away from us so that we could be 'on our own'. I wondered if in nine months' time I could persuade Mum to take me out for my birthday and not sit anywhere near me?

'Look,' said Molly, snapping me out of my thinking about the non-parental pizza party.

The screen on the GameGirl had woken up, and the Puppy Power game was ready to roll!

'Honestly, this is just so dudey,' said Molly. 'You get to choose what kind of dog you want to own, and there are all these competitions you can do to win money! When you win you can go and buy another dog. I already have two. They are called Fluffles and Midget. I mean obviously I wanted a REAL dog for my birthday, but Mum said, "No Way Ho-Zay".'

I did think a computer game was a Poor Substitute for a real dog, i.e. not as good, but I suppose if I had not had my Honey, I might possibly have thought that this toy was the best dog-type thing in the world.

'What kind of breed are they?' I asked.

'Fluffles is a miniature poodle, and Midget is a Border terrier,' she said, as they yapped and yelped and jumped up and down on the

screen. Honey's ears twitched when she heard the tiny little barks.

Who let the dogs out?

Molly had not chosen the kind of breeds that I would choose, I have to say. They were small dogs, which are not my favourite, and she had bought bows to put in their fur and weird toys like humongous beach balls and massive chewy bones that were far too big for the dogs. It was all rather over-the-top and not realistic for how a real-life owner of those kind of breeds would be.

'Watch this!' Molly shrieked. She started wibbling about how she could take the dogs for a walk in the game. 'You say "walkies" and they jump up and get all excited!'

Did someone say 'walkies'?

'See that map?' Molly said. 'Before you walk your dog, you must plan the route by drawing it on the map with the pencil thing. Then you click back to get your dog, and then you walk the dog.'

I actually thought this was really quite yawnsome. I had to drag the lead along as if I was an invisible person so the dog was walking along with this lead sort of floating above it in the air. It was der-brainish really.

And in the end it made me even more determined to persuade Mum to let Honey have real live baby poochicals of her own.

But how was I going to get Mum to agree?

That evening I lay on the sofa staring at the telly without really watching it and stroked Honey with my feet.

'I can't really believe that Mum is totally

un-persuadable,' I said in a musing sort of
way. 'After all, it was not that long ago in
the history of our family that she had said that
she would not have a dog at all! And then she
met you, gorgeous Honey-Bun . . . and now
look at us — a truly fully fledged dog-owning
family.'

Honey lifted up her head and put it in my
lap.

 I have that effect on people.

I tickled my soppy pooch's velvety ears. Surely
it was only a matter of being persistent and
thinking up some very good reasons for letting
Honey have puppies.

In circumstances such as these, I would
normally have turned to my Bestest Friend.
After all, Molly was usually the Bee's Knees
when it came to thinking up a Masterly Plan

to get me out of a crisis.
(This does not mean
that she became small and
knobbly and furry and
covered in pollen, but
that she was the best.)
But this time around,
Molly was looking distinctively
useless on the Masterly Plan front, as she was
so completely fixationed on Puppy Power. She
hadn't even asked me any questions about
Honey and the Potential Puppy Problem.

'What I need,' I told Honey, who was
looking at me with her head on one side in
a concerned and understanding fashion, 'is a
Masterly Plan of my very own to emerge out
of Thin Air and pop into my head.'

Any chance of that walk now?

5

How to Know Your Pros and Cons

On the way home from school the next day I went to the library and borrowed a copy of *Perfect Puppies* by the skilled-yet-scary dog-trainer celebrity Monica Sitstill.

If there was anyone who would have persuasive arguments about breeding and puppies and so on, it would be Ms Sitstill, the Guru of all things Dog-Related.

When I got home I took the book into the kitchen and sat down to read while I drank a cup of hot chocolate. Honey had followed me into the kitchen and was now lying under the table so I massaged her with my slipper-socked feet. It really was getting quite chilly now that the season of autumn was here, and Honey's soft fur made a lovely cosy footrest.

Those furry feet of yours aren't half bad either!

I flicked through the book, looking at the pictures of Ms Sitstill to start with. She was what Mum called a FORMIDABLE lady, which means that she was strict and bossy and ordered people around a lot – in other words, she generally got her own way. It would be nice to get *my* own way for a change, I thought. I decided to get myself a leaf out of her book and use it To My Own Advantage.

I started reading:

> Breeding from your female is a joy! It is a miracle to see new life unfolding before your eyes, and to watch Nature take its course.

This was exactly the kind of spot-on information I was looking for, I thought to myself! After all, you cannot argue with Nature.

> If, after considering all the pros and cons, you decide to go ahead with breeding, the first thing you must do is find the right mate.

This sounded sensible, I thought. I was soon so engrossed in flicking through the pages that I hardly noticed when Mum came into the kitchen with the Ironing Pile.

Mum hates ironing almost as much as I hate the eight times table. It is one of those things in life that you wonder who could have possibly invented, as it seems like the biggest waste of time imaginable.

As far as I can see, you stand there for hours, HUFFING AND pUFFING about how horrible it is, and in the end all that happens is you have a huge pile of clothes which are nice and smooth, but which will only get wrinkled again the minute you put them on. Honestly, grown-ups seem to actually *prefer* to make things complicated for themselves.

'Hi, Summer. What are you reading?' Mum asked, peering over the Mount Everest of wrinkled clothes. She was obviously PROCRASTINATING, which is a posh word I have learnt for 'wasting time instead of working/doing

something else which is more urgent'. (I love saying, 'I am PROCRASTINATING,' because

it sounds like I'm doing something important,
instead of just wasting time.)

'Nothing,' I said, quickly covering the book
with my hands.

Mum shrugged and went to get the ironing
board.

I was not yet quite ready to Bring Up
the Subject of puppies until I had all the facts
at the tips of my fingers. (It is always more
effective in a persuading situation if you do
this, I have found.)

But I felt a bit bad for not telling her
what I was doing, especially as she was so
clearly in a procrastinatory mood, so in an
effort to involve Mum a tiny bit, I called
out:

'Mum, what are Pros and Cons?'

She came back into the room, smiling. 'It
means "good things and bad things",' she said.
'Before you make a big decision, it's wise to

53

think carefully about both the good things and the bad things that could happen.'

I must have had my puzzled face on because Mum said, 'How can I explain it better . . . ? I know – imagine that you and Molly want to go to the cinema on the bus without an adult. Well, Molly's mum and I would have to weigh up the pros and cons – in other words, we would have to think about whether it was a *good* thing for you to do something so grown-up on your own, or whether in fact it would not be safe enough and therefore would be a *bad* thing.'

'Oh, I see,' I answered, going back to the book.

I personally could only see the Pros of my idea, and not any Cons. But just as I was thinking that maybe I should show Mum the book after all I ran into a list of Cons I had never even thought of:

> Matching your female dog with a suitable male
> is an art in itself and requires a lot of time, effort
> and – sometimes – money . . .

Uh-oh, I thought. Mum is seriously going to be put off the idea of Honey being a mummy if she sees the words, 'time', 'effort' and 'money' all in the same sentence. Honestly, you would think that someone might have advised Ms Sitstill not to write in such an unhelpfully scary way.

I decided to read on in the hope that eventually I would soon come to some Pros which I could use later in my very well-planned conversation with Mum.

The first top tip, or 'golden rule' as Ms Sitstill put it, was this:

1) KNOW YOUR BREED

Well, that wasn't difficult! I knew that Honey was a Golden Labrador Retriever. And I knew that she was a pure pedigree with no other type of dog in her *except* Labrador Retriever – in other words, she was not a crossbreed.

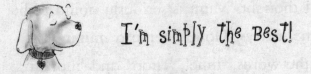

The reason I knew this for sure was that I had got her from Frank Gritter, winner of Honksome Sock Wearer of the Year Award, whose lovely pooch, Meatball (yes, that is her real name, poor thing), was Honey's mum.

2) KNOW YOUR STUD DOG

I wasn't one hundred and one per cent sure of what exactly a stud dog was. I knew that a 'stud' was a little gold thing that you had put into your earlobe when you had your ears pierced, but somehow I didn't think that dogs had to have their ears pierced before they had puppies.

How to Know Your Pros and Cons

I looked up 'stud' in the glossary:

A stud dog is the dog who will be the father of
the puppies.

Aha! I turned back to the main section, feeling
as though I was at last getting somewhere. But
what I read next filled me up with more and
more concerns of an anxious and worrisome
nature:

Is the stud a good breeding dog? Is the stud's
owner a responsible breeder?

As far as I could see, *Perfect Puppies* was asking
me more questions than it was giving me
answers! How did I know whether or not a
stud was a good breeding dog? How would I
even find a person who had such a perfect stud
dog? And how would I know all the correct and
important questions to ask the breeder when I
met him?

I sighed heavily and sank down under the table to lie next to Honey and stroke her soft velvety ears.

'What are we going to do, Honey? You'd like to be a mummy, I know you would.'

 Anything you say, just keep on with the the ear-rubbing . . .

Maybe I should ask Nick about all this? I thought. But then I realized that he would be bound to check whether or not I had asked Mum's permission, and even if I lied, he would find out from April.

I was about to fall down in the dumps with despair when I had a bLinding FLash of inspirational thinking. Unfortunately it was nearly Literally blinding, as I jumped up when I thought of it and banged my head on the table . . .

How to Know Your Pros and Cons

Frank Gritter! He would know all about how they found a proper stud dog for Meatball, AND he would be able to tell me all about how much it cost and – this was the most exciting part – he would be able to tell me how much money they had GOT for the puppies they had sold!

If Honey had puppies, we could *sell* them! Surely Mum would not say no to a money-making scheme like that? She was always moaning about how much money her daughters cost and especially how April was running around having a riot with her credit card, even though she had a job of her own, etc, etc, and on and on like that.

The Pros of this blindingly mega-brilliant flash of inspiration were obvious, I thought to myself.

The Cons were that it involved talking to

the One and Only Putrefying Pong-Meister of
Year Five: Sir Freaky-Stinky Frank Gritter the
Sock Stencher.

I love that Boy!

6

How to Ask for Assistance

On Saturday morning Nick popped over. I answered the door. I had been hovering in the hallway, trying to make up my mind whether to go over to Frank's.

'Hi, Nick!' I said. Honey ran to say hello too. Now that she's so well trained she knows she's not allowed to jump up when she is really pleased to see someone, so she just wagged her tail so hard that her bottom waggled from side to side as well.

Hey! It's the tummy-tickle man!

Nick bent down to pat Honey's head. 'No
– I'm sorry, I'm not taking you out for a walk
today, girl,' he said.

Honey sat back on her haunches, put her
head on one side and whined.

Sure I can't persuade you?

Mum came into the hall. 'Nick! We haven't
seen much of you this week – been hard at
work?'

Nick went a bit red and said, 'Er, yes.
Thanks. We're going to start looking for a
flat – did April tell you?'

Mum smiled with her mouth (but not her
eyes, I noticed) and said, 'Yes. She's in the
kitchen, if you want to go through. Come on,
Summer, let's give the lovebirds some space.'
She pushed open the sitting-room door and
nodded in the direction of the telly.

How to Ask for Assistance

I rolled my eyes to hide the fact that I was feeling embarrassed. I wished Mum wouldn't say such cringesome things about love and stuff. It always made me think of kissing. Urgh! I HATE KISSING! Not that I've ever done it, or indeed plan on ever doing it . . .

I made a big fuss of Honey so that I didn't have to say anything to Mum, who would have wanted to know why my face had gone the colour that clashes so badly with my auburn hair.

'It's all right, Mum. I think I might go out for a bit – to Frank's. OK?'

'OK,' said Mum, definitely smiling with her eyes this time. She raised her eyebrows. 'You and Frank still getting on well then?'

I huffed loudly and rolled my eyes even more. 'Mu-um!' I wailed. Honestly, that woman has lovebird nonsense on the brain, I thought.

I turned to my dog, who was the only sane person in our family. 'Come on, Honey – let's get out of this madhouse,' I whispered.

I'm sure she understood, because she became even more bottom-wiggly and bounced to the coat rack where her lead was hanging.

Walkies! At last!

I took my time walking to Frank's. I was still a bit worried that going to ask him for advice was not going to turn out to be such a good idea after all.

However, I had to admit to myself that the last time I had been truly desperate about something, it was actually Frank Gritter who had saved me in my Hour of Need – well, kind of. He'd certainly Been There For Me, as they say on telly in the dramatical bits in soap

operas. (Why they are called soap operas I have never had a faintest idea. There is never any mention of soap in them, and no one ever sings in a warbly voice like they do in real operas.)

I had in actual fact come to the rather surprising conclusion that, even though he still stank of sock-induced honksomeness, he was not that bad a person.

Honksomeness is GOOD too.

Admittedly I had had to get used to his freaky boy-language so that I could decipherate what he meant when he said things like 'Awightsummah? Yooocomintehth'par' la'ers?' (translation: 'Hello, Summer! Would you like to come along to the park later?') And I had to stand down the wind of him after Wednesday-ish, otherwise the socks he had not changed since Monday would LINGER on the breeze and make me feel distinctly Green About The Gills, which is a descriptive way of saying that it made me feel nauseatingly sick to the bottom of my boots.

Anyway, I had been feeling that going to see Frank was exactly the right thing to do, but when the moment came to actually ring his doorbell, I panicked. What if someone from school was spying on me? I could just imagine the scene in the playground on Monday morning:

Rosie Chubb: 'I saw you at Frank's yesterday!'

Others: 'WoooooOOOOOHHhhh!'

Rosie Chubb: 'What were you doing at Frank's, Summer? Is he your BOYFRIEND or something?'

She would go on and on about it forever until eternity. No, it was too hideous a thing to think about.

How to Ask for Assistance

I turned away from the front door and started to walk very quickly back down the path.

'Hello, Summer!'

Fiddlesticks. It was Frank's Mum.

'Erm, hello Mrs Gritter.'

'I saw you through the window. Come in, won't you? Hello, Honey! I'll just call Frank. He's kicking a ball around as usual . . .'

 Ball? Did someone say 'Ball'?

'Oh, right – thanks,' I said, and I walked back up the path again and into Frank's house, which as usual was very neat and tidy and not at all smelly; this never failed to completely bamboozle me. I made a mental reminder to try to find an opportunity to ask Mrs Gritter how in the high heavens above she managed to keep her house smelling so free of sock-whiff with a son like Frank around the place.

'Come through, Summer!' she called. 'Frank's in the garden and he's a bit too muddy to come in the house.'

Mud? Now that's sweet music to my floppy ears . . .

Ah! So *that's* how she dealt with the problem – she kept Frank in the garden! Great idea. I wondered if he had a kennel of his own . . .

Honey had already streaked out of the back door and was rolling around with Meatball, sniffing her bottom and doing all the disgusting things dogs do to greet each other. I was just thinking, Why on earth can't they say hello in a calm and quiet manner like humans do? when THWUMP! I was

hit on the head by a muddy football.

'AWIGH', SUMMER?' yelled Frank.
Then one of his footie mates Emerged from
the Undergrowth of the bushes and shouted,
'AWIGH'?' as well.

I was a bit annoyed as I didn't really
want to talk to Frank in front
of another stinky boy, but I
didn't exactly have a choice
now.

'Frank,' I said, calmly,
'how did you get Meatball
to have puppies?'

'Der!' said Frank,
wobbling his smelly head to
and fro and curling his lip
at me, like I was the most
der-brainish person on the planet, 'don't you
even know *that* yet? Well, first of all you get a
daddy dog, and then—'

'HAHAHAHAHA!' interrupted the honksome idiot boy next to him.

'NO! I don't mean *HOW* did she have the puppies!' I shouted, to stop him from saying anything that might be more embarrassing than the most embarrassing thing this side of Embarrassmentville. 'I meant,' I said more quietly and slowly so that this loony-tune could understand me, 'How did you *persuade* your mum to LET Meatball have puppies?'

Frank looked at me with his eyebrows creased into his forehead as if I had asked him the most difficultest maths question in the history of the entire universe. 'Er – what?' he said.

I sighed very over-dramatically and turned my back on him and his friend with my arms crossed. 'Fine. I can see that you are not actually behaving like a real live human being today and that you are in fact on Planet Zorg,

70

How to Ask for Assistance

so I will leave you to do whatever it is Alien
Life Forms like doing on a Saturday, and I
will find some more intelligenter life forms to
converse with,' I said very importantly and,
feeling really quite pleased with myself, I called
Honey and marched out of the garden.

AWWWWW! But the fun's only
just Begun . . .

'Leaving already, Summer?' said Mrs Gritter as
I came into the kitchen. 'Won't you stay for
a snack? Bunny always has a biscuit
around this time,' she added,
opening a packet.
BUNNY? Was that her
nickname for Mr Stink-i-verse?
HAHAHAHAHA! That's a useful
bit of information I can store up my
sleeve, I thought.

71

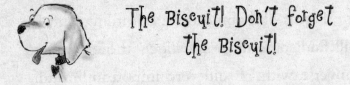

The Biscuit! Don't forget the Biscuit!

'Thank you, Mrs Gritter,' I said in my most politest of voices. 'Those biscuits *do* look delicious. Unfortunately I have to go home now. Thank you for having me.'

Frank had appeared in the doorway at this point. He obviously had his biscuit radar-smell-o-vision on.

BIIIISKIIITTTT!

'Cn'av a biscuit, Mum?' Frank asked, grinning muddily.

UUUHHHH . . .

Mrs Gritter handed him the plate. 'Bunny, I

How to Ask for Assistance

hope you haven't upset Summer,' she said. 'She seems to be leaving already.'

For a split of a moment I thought Frank looked a tiny bit guilty, but then his smelly mate appeared at his side and Frank blurted out, 'She's just got her knickers in a twist cos her mum won't let Honey have puppies.'

His mate guffawed with biscuity laughter.

I felt my face do its ultra-red thing and panicked that I might actually burst into tears in front of those disgusting examples of the male species. So I hastily grinned at Mrs Gritter through my grinding teeth and muttered, 'Thanks for nothing, Frank,' while making the quickest exit that was humanly possible with my dog lunging at the biscuit plate.

73

So that was that, on the Masterly Plan front, as far as Frank Gritter was concerned.

The Biscuits were great though!

7

How to Stop a Conversation in Its Tracks

After the completely useless time spent at Frank's house, I decided I would have to Take my Chance and Get Straight to the Point with Mum.

Maybe if I reminded her that Nick would help us out, as he'd said, she would come around to my way of thinking, I told myself.

Still, I couldn't face talking to her that weekend, and instead I waited until Monday after school.

Unfortunately, that Monday Mum wasn't

in the sort of mood to come around to anyone's way of thinking when she got in. For a start she was late.

'That *stupid* man I have to share an office with just would not shut up tonight!' she wailed as she stomped around the kitchen, opening and shutting cupboards and slamming down packets of food.

Someone's Bark is Worse than Their Bite . . .

Honey and I skulked out of the room to wait until Mum had come out of Work Mode, even though I felt as if my brain was pushing against the sides of my skull with all the puppy-related conversation I was desperate to talk about.

But I had learned my lesson about tackling tricky conversation subjects with Mum. There

was utterly no point in bringing up anything important the minute she walked through the door. She was always quite tired and grumpy and more than likely to say 'No Way Ho-Zay' to things without even thinking. Like the time I had been completely desperate for a pair of those shoes with wheels in that make you look as if you are hovering above the ground. They are so mega-cool and funkster. Molly has some, and so does Rosie Chubb (except it would take more than a pair of those shoes to make it look as if that hippopotamus was hovering – something like a forklift truck might do the trick . . .) and I had been DESᵖERAᵗE to have a pair too. In fact I had been *too* desperate, which had the effect that my brain lost all its CAPACITIES for thinking before it acted. So instead of waiting patiently until Mum was ready to listen to a calm and well-thought-through argument, my brain went into

11

overdrive and my mouth BLURTED oUt some words before I could stop it, and those words were: 'So can I have those wheelie shoes, or not?'

I never did get a pair.

So this time I just waited as patiently as I could without chewing the insides of my cheeks off. Mum eventually made a cup of tea, and then we went into the sitting room and sat on the sofa and I thought, She MUST have had time to relax by now.

In any case, I couldn't wait any longer to bring up the important and frankly quite scarisome topic which was playing doolally weirdo things with my mind, so I Took The Plunge:

'Mu-um?'

'Hmmm?' said Mum, slurping her tea.

'Have you thought any more about what Nick said about Honey?' I decided to start

in this most cryptical of ways so that I didn't have to say the word 'puppies' out loud and put Mum off in the first five seconds of the conversation. Honey sat up as if she was listening too.

Did someone say my name?

'Hmmm,' said Mum, putting her mug down and patting Honey absent-mindedly.

'And?' I said. Mum was obviously going to need a bit of PROMPTING, which is a way of saying that she needed a bit of help getting going with this conversation. In other words, I wished she would say something other than 'Hmmm'.

'The answer is . . . no,' said Mum quietly.

'S-s-sorry?' I whimpered, closing my eyes in utter non-believing-ness.

'NO!' said Mum, not so quietly. 'Summer,

when are you going to learn that nagging
me and going on and on about something is
simply not going to work? I have had the most
hideous day at work with that IDIOT of a
man wittering on in my left ear all day, and I
come home to put my feet up and have a quiet
cup of tea to find that I have my daughter
wittering on in my right ear about PUPPIES!'

I guessed that was a pretty clear answer.

'Oh,' I said, opening my eyes and biting
my lip.

Then Mum puffed out a long breath of
air and gave me a saddish look and said,
'Oh, Summer, please don't be disappointed.
You know puppies are a lot of work, even if
we would only have them in the house for a
couple of months. I am *so* busy with work these
days, and you've got more homework, and
if April's going to move out she wouldn't be
around to help either.'

How to Stop a Conversation in Its Tracks

I was just about to resort to my absolutely last resort-ish solution which was to just look at Mum as Pleadingly and Sorrowfully as I possibly could . . .

Impressive puppy-dog eyes you've got there!

. . . when—

This CRUCIAL (in other words mega-important) moment was Rudely Interrupted by the sounds of things being SMASHED and broken outside our house. Mum and I leaped up from our chairs in shock and Honey started barking.

Whooaaa! Intruder alert!

'Stay here, Summer,' Mum hissed, her eyebrows scrunched into the middle of her forehead in a concerned and slightly frightened manner.

'Mum! Don't go out there!' I cried. 'It might be a burglar!'

But then we heard the words, 'How could you do this to me?' in a highly screechisome voice that was impossible not to recognize, and then there was another—

Mum and I glanced at each other warily and then we both tiptoed to the sitting-room window to peek out cautiously. Honey was hot on our heels.

Wouldn't miss this for the world!

How to Stop a Conversation in Its Tracks

The scene that we saw would have been quite literally amusing if it had not been quite so literally terrifying.

Outside our house was a quite Scary Mary of a person in what can only be described as a Torrent of Rage, throwing milk bottles at the pavement. This person had very DISHEVELLED hair, which means it was all over the place as if it had gone through a bush backwards – in other words it was a mess – their face was a deeply strange purply colour and their eyes were ringed with so much black stuff they looked like the Creature from the Swampy Lagoon or something similar.

Whimper

It was April. With Nick. And the Bottom Shuffler!

April was doing what Molly would call

Making A Scene, which does not mean
that she was being filmed for an extremely
glamorous Hollywood movie. It means that
she was screaming and shouting so loudly that
people would start staring if we did not get her
inside as Quick As A Flash.

'Stay here, Summer,' said Mum again, and
she dashed outside.

I sat in the window with Honey, waiting to
see what Mum would do.

Go get that scary monster!

Mum went up to April and started talking to her, and then she talked to Nick and the Bottom Shuffler as well. They all followed her back into the house.

A feeling of utter nervousness swept through me like a giant wave. What was going on?

The front door closed quietly and I heard Mum say, 'I'll make us all some tea and we can talk about this calmly.' She sounded as though she was talking to some frightened animals rather than a bunch of grown-ups who had had an argument.

I tiptoed to the kitchen to watch the Proceedings Unfold. (In fact I sort of hid in the doorway like a spy.)

'Now,' said Mum, 'why don't you tell me what's going on?'

Nick was staring at the floor. The Bottom Shuffler was staring at Mum, her hands on her hips and a Look of Insolence on her face. She flicked her hair (which was not in a ponytail today, I noticed) and said, 'Nothing.'

April glared at the Bottom Shuffler. So did Honey.

GRRRRR . . .

Then April's face went crumply, her already very smeary eyes went watery and she started to blub in a very un-April-type way.

'That idiot has been cheating on me,' she squeaked in a HICCUpY fashion, pointing at Nick. 'WITH HER!' she added, pointing at the Bottom Shuffler.

'Wha—?' Mum and I said in UNISON – in other words, together.

Mum turned and spotted me in my Hidden

How to Stop a Conversation in Its Tracks

Spy position, but luckily for me she was too shocked to tell me to go away.

'He's a 🙈✱☉‼✱☉ ❓ ❓❓⁉🙈☉'!' said April. It was too impossibly rude of her and I will never tell anyone what she actually called him.

'Is this true?' Mum asked Nick. He looked up and his face was red and upset-looking. 'Listen, Angela—' he started.

'OF COURSE IT'S TRUE!' April howled. 'I SAW THEM TOGETHER WITH MY OWN EYES!' Her eyes didn't look as if they would be able to see anything much just at that moment. They were severely red, and the blackness around them had started running down her face.

'Darling,' said the Bottom Shuffler, rolling her eyes like Molly does when I've said something der-brainish, 'don't you think you're being just a *teensy* bit paranoid? Just because your boyfriend and I work together and go out and have a bit of lunch together, and just because he

87

sometimes gives me a lift home after work — it doesn't mean you need to overreact like this!'

'I NEVER OVERREACT!' April screamed.

'Listen, dear,' said Mum, backing away slightly. 'I'm sure there's a perfectly reasonable explanation for all this.'

'Yes, and the "perfectly reasonable explanation" is that SHE has STOLEN MY BOYFRIEND!' April yelled. 'I saw them at lunchtime — she had HER ARM through HIS ARM, and they were LAUGHING! And then I go to meet him after work and SHE is in HIS CAR!' April added, glaring at Mum, as though it was all her fault.

'Well, I don't think that proves anything—' Mum said.

'I'm sorry,' said the Bottom Shuffler — and for one moment I thought she was apologizing to April — 'but I've got to get out of this madhouse. Come on, Nick. Didn't you say there

How to Stop a Conversation in Its Tracks

was a heap of paperwork to go through tonight? We can do it at my place if you like.' And she blinked at him. That woman has severely bad problems with her eyes, I thought once again.

Nick muttered something I couldn't quite hear and then looked at April with the sort of pleading puppy-dog expression I was using on Mum only minutes earlier.

But they had the same effect on April that they had on Mum, i.e. No Effect Whatsoever.

'Yes, you'd better go round to HER place, hadn't you, Nick?' she hissed.

And so Nick followed the Bottom Shuffler out of our house.

April sank down on to a chair and buried her face in her hands. It was like watching a balloon go 'bleurgh' after all the air has whooshed out of it.

Mum and I glanced at each other and let out a lot of air ourselves, which was a relief as I think I had not breathed at all during the argument.

None of this made even one TIYCHICAL SpECK of sense to me: Nick going out with the Bottom Shuffler? Nick already had a girlfriend with long blonde hair who filed her nails and giggled down the phone, so why on earth would he be interested in *another* girlfriend who looked and acted exactly the same? Surely if you had fallen out of love with someone, you would not go and fall straight into love with someone else who looked and sounded exactly the same as the *last* person that you had been in love with?

I decided I had to say something.

'Er . . . April, don't you think you might have made a mistake? After all, Nick is such a nice man. Maybe the Bott— nurse and he had to do some very important work together at lunchtime, and maybe he had to tell her lots of

How to Stop a Conversation in Its Tracks

important vet-related business that they don't have time for during normal office-surgery-working hours . . .' I had started to speak faster and faster and was in danger of having what Molly calls VERBAL DIARRHOEA which is a rather disgusting way of saying that words were flowing out of my mouth at top speed in an unstoppable kind of way.

Verbal = Diarrhoea = Words

'Summer,' Mum hissed, putting her hand on my sleeve, 'I think you should take Honey into the garden for a second.'

But I was in a full flow of quick panic-talking and I carried on: '– If you like, Molly and I could ask him about it when we next go and see him about Honey, and I'm sure you'll find it's all a misunderstanding—'

'NOOOOOOOOOOOOO!' April shrieked.

Honey jumped back and yelped. So did I.

 She's freaking me out!

April was now actually pulling at her hair like a demented witch-type person. 'You are never to go near him EVER again! You will have to get a new vet for Honey. I don't want to hear that man's name mentioned in our house from this day forward!' she added, stomping out of the room and up to her bedroom in a way that was very over-dramatical, even for April.

A new vet for Honey? But if Nick was not our vet any more, there was No Way Ho-Zay in a million trillion years that I would ever get Mum to say 'yes' to Honey having puppies.

My Verbal Diarrhoea had stopped. There was nothing more to be said.

Phew, she's gone.

8

How to Sink into a Pit of Despair

The next day I dragged my feet so slowly that I missed the bus and had to drag my extremely slow-moving feet all the way to school. I was nearly there when I heard someone running and panting behind me. I was not really in the mood to talk to anyone so I kept my head down and carried on dragging myself to the school gates.

'Hey! Wait for me!'

It was Molly!

'How come you are so late?' she panted, catching up with me and stopping. She bent over and clutched her sides. 'Ooh, I've got a stitch,' she said.

Why people say this, I have no idea. A stitch is a pattern you make with a needle and thread on a piece of cloth. What has that got to do with having a pain in your tummy when you've been running? Or maybe it means that it *feels* as though someone has sewn through your tummy with a needle and thread . . .

'You're late too,' I pointed out, a little bit grumpily.

'Yeah,' said Molly, standing up again and grinning at me a bit like a loony. 'I stayed up too late last night getting to the next level in the agility trials on Puppy Power, so I overslept this morning. Listen, I'm sorry I didn't call you

last night, but this game is soooo ADDICTIVE
– in other words, I just can't stop play— hey,
what's up?'

I'm ashamed to say that Molly rabbiting
on and on about her puppy game just felt a bit
like the last straw and my eyes had gone rather
leaky of their own accord.

'Nothing,' I muttered, angrily rubbing them.

'Oh no, I've upset you, haven't I?' Molly
said, suddenly looking really quite anxious and
concerned, which is not a look she has that
often.

I sniffed and shook my head. 'It's not you,'
I said, which was kind of partly true anyway.
'It's Mum, and April and . . . and Honey's not
going to have puppies now and it's all Nick's
fault!' I sobbed out the last part and went a bit
HICCUpY just like my sister had done the
night before.

'What?' said Molly, looking confused

95

now. She linked her arm into mine and we started walking towards school as the bell for registration rang.

I told Molly everything that had happened and ended with a quite full-on impression of April screaming like the Creature from the Swampy Lagoon.

Up until that point Molly had listened very sympathetically, but when it came to my (even though I say so myself, extremely realistic) impression of my loonitistical sister, Molly's face changed from Caring and Concerned to Giggly and Hysterical.

And of course that set me off too.

We were both seeing a quite hilarious picture of my sister in my head, and all we could do was laugh about it. This kind of thing happens quite a lot when you are the Bestest Friends in the Universe and you find yourself on the very exact same length of brainwave.

How to Sink into a Pit of Despair

So that is how we both came to be walking through the playground, laughing the tops of our heads off and doing impressions of April, just as our form teacher, Mrs Wotherspoon, came out of the headteacher's office.

'Oh, so we think it's highly amusing to miss registration, do we?' she squawked.

Not for the first time I sighed inside my head and wished with all my heart that we were still in Year Four with Mr Elgin. Mr Elgin had been annoying in a mild sort of teachery way and would say doolally things like: 'You have two ears and one mouth, use them in that proportion,' and 'Do I have to say everything twice?' and 'Act your age, not your shoe size' (which never made any sense to me, as I was nine at the time and my feet were size twelve, so surely he should have said, 'Act your shoe size and not your age'). But apart from this, he was actually quite nice, and he had even arranged for the Talent Contest which Molly, Honey and I had won hands (and paws) down.

Mrs Wotherspoon was in a completely different CATEGORY of teacherliness. After our first day in her class Molly had said, 'If Mrs Wotherspoon was a dog, she'd be a Dobermann pinscher,' (which is not a dog that belongs in the lovely, cuddly bracket of poochiness at all). She was tall and spindly-

looking, as if she would get blown over in the lightest of summer breezes, but this does not mean that she was gentle. Oh no! When she spoke you realized that she was spiky and fierce and probably had a Grip of Iron like the Bottom Shuffler. Her facial features were, as Molly said, 'so sharp that if someone put a handle on them they would turn into a knife', her eyes were like those glassy eyes you get on old-fashioned teddy bears and dolls, and worst of all her fingers were the longest and spideriest I had ever seen. Personally I was convinced she was a witch, but Molly said she couldn't be as she didn't have a Familiar.

'A familiar what?' I had asked.

'You know, a cat or something,' Molly said.

'Oh,' I had said, nodding wisely, but inside my brain I was thinking, What in the name of all things sane is a Familiar Cat? One you have got to know particularly well, perhaps? In that case, is Honey my Familiar Dog? And does that make me a witch?

'Are you going to stand there all morning gawping like a goldfish with rigor mortis, Summer Love?' Mrs Wotherspoon said, dragging me back into the

99

present situation by the terrifying screechiness of her crone-type speaking.

'N-no,' I stammered, making a mental reminder of the word 'riggermortiss' and thinking that I must look it up in the dictionary.

'Good,' snapped Mrs W. 'I won't bother asking you and your sidekick here the reason for your appalling lateness, but let me make one thing abundantly clear: if it happens again, you will be spending every break time from here to the end of eternity picking up the litter in the playground. Do you understand me?'

Molly and I nodded silently and tried desperately hard not to look at each other in case we started giggling again. Mrs W.'s voice is so completely freaky that it often makes us nearly wet ourselves with laughter once she gets going on something.

'Good,' she said again. 'Well, hurry along

to the hall. We have already started the English lesson. Everyone is ready to show the work they've done on the scenes from *Romeo and Juliet*. I hope you have at least done your homework?'

'Oh no!' hissed Molly as we followed Mrs W. on her clicky heels. 'I forgot to do it!'

I hissed back, 'So did I!'

Mrs W. did not even turn round. 'That's a shame, girls. I shall have to pair you up with some people who *have* done their homework, shan't I?'

I didn't think life could throw anything else at me that could possibly make me feel any worse and fall further down into the Pit of Despair which was where I was right at that very moment.

We arrived in the hall to find that everyone had taken advantage of Mrs W. not being with them to do what Mum would call Run Riot

– in other words, they were chasing each other round the place, climbing on the wall bars that we use for gym and screeching like monkeys at a rather EXUBERANT tea party.

'SILENCE!' Mrs W. screamed.

It was like a quite scary version of musical statues. Everyone stopped in the mid-tracks of what they were doing. The people on the wall bars looked particularly shaky.

'I am beginning to think that teaching serious literature to you lot is rather like trying to get a fish to sing the national anthem,' Mrs W. spluttered. 'I really don't think William Shakespeare would approve of all these shenanigans.'

I didn't know what shenanigans were, but judging by the kind of language this Shakespeare person used in his olde worlde daye, I personally

thought he would probably like shenanigans very much indeed.

'Molly,' Mrs W. continued, 'I would like you to pair up with Rosie. She doesn't appear to have a partner yet.' I wonder why, I thought. 'Summer, you can go with Frank Gritter. He is one person at least who seems to know what he is doing this morning.'

It seemed that the Pit of Despair had reached new depths of Despairedness.

'Now, Frank, you had chosen to work on the balcony scene, hadn't you?' Mrs W. was saying. 'I want you to think yourself into the character. Think love. Think romance.'

Oh my goodness dearie me. I wanted to die there on the very spot, but as I knew from the film, that didn't happen to Juliet until some time after the balcony scene. I pulled a face at Frank as if to say, 'I know this is horrendous, but it wasn't my idea.' I thought Frank would

103

roll his eyes or something to show me that he agreed, but instead he just winked at me. I nearly groaned out loud. This really was the end of everything. Life would never be worth living ever again. I would never smile or laugh or run through the spring flowers with a pooch on a lead in my whole long miserable life.

'Stop leering like that, Gritter. You are supposed to woo the girl!' Mrs W. demanded.

'OK,' said Frank, with a distinctively mischievous look in his eye. 'Like this?' and he got down on one knee

How to Sink into a Pit of Despair

and held one hand to his heart and the other out to me as if he was going to ask me to marry him or something.

I thought I was going to be sick, so I closed my eyes tightly and prepared for total and utter Public Humiliation of the hugest degree. Then I heard a very strange noise.

'Woooo! Woooo!'

Everyone in the class exploded into raucous and uproarious laughter and I opened my eyes to see the expression on Mrs W.'s face. Now she was the one who looked like a goldfish with rigorous ortis.

I did the only thing a girl could do in such a situation. I giggled so hard I left the Despairedness behind.

9

How to Have a Girls' Night In

'**W**e have to think of something,' I said to Molly on the way to the bus that afternoon. It was getting darker earlier in the evenings now so we were not allowed to walk home unfortunately. It left less time for chatting, but at least it was warmer.

'What are you two gossiping about?'

Frank had caught up with us.

Oh no, I thought. Just because I laughed at his Wooooing, he now thinks I will allow him to hang around with me.

'Nothing that concerns you, Frank Gritter,'

x

said Molly in her best mature-type way of speaking. Then she turned to me. 'We just need a Masterly Plan to beat the most masterly of masterly ones we've ever come up with before,' she said carelessly.

'You make it sound so easy,' I grumbled, doing my best to avoid Eye Contact with Mr Stinko-Pants, 'but it's not. We've only had to solve one problem at a time before. Now we've got to think of a way of getting April and Nick back together – otherwise I don't have a vet for Honey and her puppies – AND we've got to find a way to get Mum to agree to breed from Honey in the first place.'

I saw Frank from out of the corner of my eye. He was definitely listening in on my private conversation with my Bestest Friend. The sneak. He might be funny sometimes, but he's still an annoying smelly boy, I thought irritably.

107

Puppy Power

'Don't worry, Summer,' Molly said in her soothingest Best Friend voice (although the effect was not as good as it should have been, as she was waving a half-munched doughnut at me as she spoke). 'We just need to tackle one thing at a time. That's what Puppy Power says about dog training! In fact, only last night when I was getting to the next level on the agility I found out—'

'Molly,' I said, 'I don't think Puppy Power is going to be much use in sorting out my particular problems. April and Nick aren't badly behaved dogs, are they? They are just stupid humans who are making an embarrassingly and frankly annoyingly big deal about the fact that they have fallen out of love.'

'OK, OK,' said Molly, harrumphing a bit.

'Hey!' I said, suddenly having a huge brainwave that threatened to Knock My Socks

How to Have a Girls' Night In

Off with its brilliance. 'You know when you and I had a Falling Out?'

'Ye-es,' said Molly, sounding like she wasn't sure my brainwave was going to Knock *Her* Socks Off.

'Well, we Made Up again after Falling Out, didn't we?' I continued, without giving Molly a chance to disagree. 'And we did it quite simply by having a water-fight and eating a lot of ice cream.'

'Ye-es,' said Molly again.

'So, we could Engineer it so that Nick has to come round to see Honey, and when he arrives we start a water-fight, and once he and April have had a bit of fun with the hose and everything, we could serve them some Knickerbocker Glories.'

'Great idea in theory,' said Molly slowly,

looking at me as if I had just landed from **Planet Idiocy**, 'but hadn't you noticed that it's autumnal-ish? A bit cold for water-fights, if you ask me. Also, correct me if I'm wrong, but I'm not sure that Nick and April aren't just a little bit too old for a water-fight—'

'All right!' I stormed. 'So you think of something better!'

'Erm, mind if I butt in a second?' said Frank, grinning like a master-maniac from ear to dirty ear.

'Yes!' Molly and I said in Unison.

Frank Ploughed On Regardless as if we'd just spoken in Russian or something. 'I think I may have an easier and less freezing solution to your little problem.'

'Oh, listen to Frank Gritter, the Guru Romantic Problem Solver!' Molly crowed. 'Sorry, Frank, I had forgotten that you were such an Expert in helping people with their

110

love lives. You've learned it all from your in-depth studies of *Romeo and Juliet*, I suppose?'

Frank narrowed his eyes at Molly. 'If you're not interested in what I've got to say, then fine,' he said in an I-don't-care-what-you-think manner of speaking.

A tiny light bulb of interest went on inside my head and I thought, Maybe Frank has come up with a Masterly Plan of his own!

'What *have* you got to say then?' I asked, as if I didn't really want to know.

Frank carried on being a devil who couldn't care less. 'No, no, it's quite clear that you don't need *me* to interfere in one of your Masterly Plans. I mean, who am I – a mere boy – to offer you assistance?'

'Oh for heaven's sake, Frank Gritter, spit it out!' Molly said in her most fiercesome-ist tone of talking.

111

Puppy Power

Frank raised one of his eyebrows in the James Bond-ish manner he sometimes has and said, 'No, it's OK. Actually, the more I come to think of it, no woman could possibly understand the brilliance of my idea.'

'What in the high heavens do you know about what women can and can't understand—?' Molly started in her indignatious way, but I cut in quickly:

'Come on, Molly. It is quite obvious that Frank Gritter does not know his armpit from his elbow – in other words, he has not one iota of an idea of what he is talking about. Let's go home.'

I couldn't help wondering though . . .

I was still wondering when I got home, to find Mum was already there, and was unpacking some severely interesting-looking shopping bags.

How to Have a Girls' Night In

'I thought we were overdue for a girls' night in,' Mum said, giving me a hug. Honey bounded up and licked me on the hand.

 I smell yummy snacks!

'Great,' I said, ESPYING some popcorn and marshmallows peeking out of the top of the bags.

If it hadn't been for the interesting-looking shopping bags, I might have had something else to say about the basic CONCEPT of a Girls' Night In. Frankly I am always having girls' nights in, as that is what life as a ten-year-old is all about, it seems, i.e. I am a girl and I am always in at night because I am apparently too young to go out (unless you count going round to Molly's house, which is hardly going out as we always stay in). My sister April can go GALLIVANTING about till all hours, flicking her long blonde hair and snogging her boyfriend (well, when she has one) while I have to stay in and do MARATHON-STYLE homework sessions and go to bed early. Not that I would prefer to be flicking my hair and I certainly would NOT be snogging anyone, all of which is a certifiably INSANE waste of a good night out, it seems to me. If I could go out gallivanting, I would take Molly with me and we would eat pizza and chips and ice cream and watch three films in a row and stay up till at least midnight and generally PAINT THE TOWN RED. (Although we might get arrested for that last bit, as that can, I think, be classed as a crime of a graffiti-ing-type nature.)

'Do you want to ask Molly to join us?' Mum asked.

I pulled a fed-up face, which is when my mouth goes tight and ski-whiff and I frown a

bit. 'No. She's too busy learning how to wash her dogs on Puppy Power or something.'

'Right,' said Mum.

'Er – is April joining us?' I asked a bit warily. I didn't really want to spend an evening with the Wailing Monster of the Black Lagoon, even if I did feel a bit sorry for her. She had hardly spoken a word or eaten a thing since seeing Nick with the Bottom Shuffler, and even though Nick kept phoning and asking to speak to her, she wouldn't talk to him.

Mum proceeded to unload the kind of PLETHORA of goodies (in other words, monster-mega-huge amounts) that are normally associated with birthdays or Christmasses.

'No, she's having a Girls' Night Out actually,' Mum said. 'Girls always stick together when they've got boyfriend trouble –' Thanks, Mum – **Information Overload**! I do not want to talk about Boyfriend Trouble.

'– I thought you and I could do with spending some quality mother-and-daughter time together, that's all.' Then she added: 'By the way, I saw Frank today.'

And she winked.

Why, oh why, had everyone started winking at me all the time! First Frank, now Mum . . . And why did she have to wink after saying Frank's name? Argh! Mortification Level one thousand and thirteen! Thank the high heavens that Molly wasn't coming round for this famous Girls' Night In if Mum was going to behave like this!

I suddenly had a horror-struck moment of utter cringeworthiness.

'Mum . . . this mother/daughter/quality-time thing . . . it's not cos you want to have a heart-to-heart with *me* about . . . er . . . boys and stuff, is it?' I asked.

Mum laughed. (At least she didn't look sad

any more.) 'No! Why would I want to waste a perfectly good girls' night in talking about something as boring as *that*?' she asked.

Phew.

'So what's with all the treats then?' I asked.

'Because I thought you might like to watch . . . this!' Mum cried, pulling out one more item with a flourishy hand movement. 'Ta-daaa!' she sang out.

It was a DVD. With a picture on the cover of the most gorgeousest golden Labrador ever in the entire universe (well, OK, not as GORGEoUSƖY SCRUmpƬUƖICIoUS as Honey) and she was surrounded by smaller and just as cute and delumptious PUPPIES!

Oh. My. Goodness.

'Don't get too excited,' Mum said. But she was grinning like an over-excited loop-the-loop loony insane person herself.

Puppy Power

'Eeeee!' I yelled and launched myself at Mum, knocking packets of crisps and popcorn flying in all directions. Mostly in the direction of Honey, as it happened.

Things are looking up . . .

'I don't know what you've been saying to Frank,' Mum said, looking at me with narrowed eyes, but still smiling, 'but he said he thought we'd enjoy watching this.'

I almost gasped aloud. Was *this* the Masterly Plan that Frank had tried to tell me about that afternoon? Maybe, just maybe, that boy was OK after all.

Mum and I got ourselves comfy. We put a big bowl of popcorn on the little table in front of us. Then we dimmed the lights, sat

back with our mini-tubs of toffee-fudge ice cream and relaxed. Mum put the DVD on and I snuggled up to her. She kind of sighed and hugged me tight with her free arm. 'This is great, Summer. We must have more nights like this before you get too old and sophisticated,' she said.

But my eyes were already fixated one hundred and ten per cent on the screen. There were all kinds of tips and hints about talking to breeders and finding the right male dog for your female dog to have puppies with. The narrator was a breeder who had shown her dogs at Crufts and other mega-important shows like that all over the world. She talked to the camera about her dogs and she also interviewed a vet.

'He's not as nice as Nick, is he?' I said to Mum.

'Hmm,' she said, sadly.

Then I felt a bit sad too, thinking that Nick might never be our vet again. But soon the DVD got more exciting, and I got distractivated away from my sad thoughts – thank the high heavens for that.

The vet was talking about how to prepare the whelping box, which is basically the bed in which the puppies will be born and spend the first few weeks of their life.

'It doesn't look like they need that much space to start with, does it?' said Mum. 'Hey, Honey – do you want to be a mummy?' she added, ruffling Honey's fur.

Whatever you say — just keep on ruffling.

My heart did a leapy thing as if it was trying to escape out through my mouth. I choked on my popcorn which was probably a good thing – otherwise I might have SQUEALED with excitement. I had to stay calm.

The DVD was, I have to say, the best thing I have ever watched in my whole life on a telly screen. Even better than Monica Sitstill's dog-agility training programme, *Pup Idol,* or Molly's and my old favourite, *Seeing Stars.* I learned so much about how to find the right breeder, how to get your dog's hips and eyes checked to make sure she's healthy and how to prepare your home for when the mother gives birth. I was so captivated by the information and the beautiful puppies on the screen that I did not

121

look at Mum one single time . . . until it got to the bit where the puppies were born. They were so unbelievably tiny and so squidgy and snuffly that I was overwhelmingly transfixated.

'Oooh! Ahhh! They are SOOOOO cute!' I said, and turned to look at Mum.

First of all I thought she looked cross. Her face was pink and she was sort of frowning at the telly. Then I thought, Oh no, she is going to say that this DVD was the worst idea in the world and that Frank is a stupid idiot der-brain for lending it to us and that there is no way in one hundred thousand million zillion years that Honey will ever have—

'Oh, Summer,' Mum said quietly.

'Ye-es,' I answered, also quietly, and trying not to look at Mum. I was waiting for the worst.

'Darling,' she said, sniffing a bit, 'you know I said that I wasn't ready for Honey to have puppies?'

'Hmmm?' I said, not daring for one tiny bit of a moment to say anything else.

'And you know I said I thought it would be too much work for us?'

'Hmmmmmm.'

'Well . . . this is becoming a bit of a habit of mine where dogs are concerned, but – I've changed my mind!'

'Wha-a-aaaa?' I said in a not very ELOQUENT tone of speaking.

'I just can't resist those little babies,' said Mum stroking Honey's head as she watched the pups on the screen.

I threw my arms around Mum and hugged her tight. 'Yiiippppeeee!' I cried. 'Mum – you've just made my dreams come true!'

Honey was going to be a MUMMY!

 Who's the mummy?

10

How to Get Seriously Fed Up

The next day I found myself doing a very unusual thing. I ran up to Frank outside school and tapped him on the shoulder.

'Wotcha, Juliet!' he said, turning round and winking at me.

Argh! I wished he would stop that winking thing. And as for calling me 'Juliet' – just because I was grateful to him for getting Mum to change her mind, it did not mean that I wanted to be connected with him in THAT way in any shape or form, even in a make-believe play-type situation.

How to Get Seriously Fed Up

'Mum wants to know about the breeder you used for Meatball,' I said, ignoring his unamusingness.

'OK, I'll get my mum to call yours later.'

I didn't know if I could survive a whole day of the nine times table and what happens to water when it reaches 100°C, but somehow I did.

$5 \times 9 = 45$

$3 \times 9 = 27$

$8 \times 9 = 72$

$9 \times 9 = 81$

At last it was the evening, and Mum was telling me the details of her conversation with Mrs Gritter.

'They used a breeder who is apparently an amazing man,' Mum told me. 'It seems that what he doesn't know about dogs isn't worth knowing.' Mum was getting all sparkly-eyed, and I was trying not to squeak with excitement. 'Mrs Gritter is going to arrange for us to meet him this weekend. She says he's a dog whisperer — he actually seems to know the Inner Workings of a dog's mind!'

'Yippeee!' I cried, flinging my arms around Mum's neck.

Mum gave me a squeeze and gently peeled my arms off her so that she could breathe. 'She also said it would be a good idea to get a vet to come along with us.'

My heart sank a bit.

'But we haven't got a vet at the moment,' I pointed out. Nick was, after all, not exactly Popular Person Number One these days, what with April still being totally convinced

that he was now Going Out with the Bottom Shuffler. In fact, not only had he not been seen in the nearby VICINITY of our house for days and days, he had stopped phoning too.

Mum smiled and said, 'Yes, we have — Honey's still registered with Nick. April doesn't need to know. Anyway, I've had an idea,' she said, most cryptically. 'You might not be the only one whose dreams come true . . .'

The rest of the week turned out to be a very slow period of time in my life. I could not concentrate on a single thing at school as all I could think about was Honey and whether she would like the boy dog that would be the father of her pups and whether she would get pregnant right away and how many puppies she would have and what colour they would be . . .

And I have to say that Molly was not one

127

single speck of a bit of help during that time either, as all she wanted to talk about was Puppy Power. One night I invited her round for tea, and she brought her mega-annoying game with her. We were sitting in the Den with Honey, and I was telling Molly how excited and nervous I was about going to the breeder at the weekend, and she wasn't even listening to me.

'Look at this!' said Molly, touching the screen of her game with the plastic pen thing. 'It's soooo dudey! You can wash the dogs — much easier than washing a real dog, as it's not messy to do. You don't have to tie them to a tree and race around with a hose and get soaking wet In The Process, that's for sure!'

 Where's the fun in that?

I sort of winced inside when Molly said this,

128

as it felt a tiny bit like a criticism. Honey had been a nightmare to wash until I managed to successfully and brilliantly train her. I had had more than a person's fair share of being soaked right through to the skin and bone while hosing her down.

'I've taken Fluffles to the shower room!' she squeaked. 'Here, hold the stylus,' she said, handing me the pen thing. 'Now, see that little sponge? Put the pencil on the sponge and rub Fluffles with it.'

I did what she said and all this soapy foam stuff appeared. Oh my goodness dearie me, this was the most der-brainish of der-brained games in the history of the world. Fluffles was actually grinning! As if a dog can actually grin in real life . . .

'OK, now Fluffles is all soapy, get that shower-head thing at the top there,' said Molly.

I sighed heavily as a Big Hint that I was

129

finding the whole thing rather wearisome, but did as Molly said and dragged the shower-head down to Fluffles. Sparkly water came out of it and cleaned the foam off. It was Yawnsville Central.

'Dudey!' Molly yelled, and collapsed backwards, howling with hysterical giggle-laughter.

After washing Fluffles and Midget about thirty-eight times each, Molly finally said it was time to switch the game off as it was running out of batteries. Thank the high heavens. I was getting seriously fed up with those grinning fluffy computer-pooches.

Also I was getting seriously fed up with hearing the word 'dudey' so much.

11
How to Choose Your Breeder

At last the weekend of Total and Complete BLiss and Excitement arrived. On the day in question I got up extra-mega-specially early and laid out a celebratory going-to-the-breeder's breakfast (chocolatey croissants, orange juice and the Elements and Ingredients for the making of hot chocolate).

Molly came round to have breakfast with us. She had told me that there was No-Way Ho-Zay in a million and one years that she was going to let me go to the breeders without some Moral Support from her.

'We have to keep your mum On Side,' she whispered when she arrived. 'If there is even the slightest glimmer of a hint that your mum is going to change her mind, we have to be prepared with lots of helpful tips and facts to keep her focused.'

'Why are you suddenly so interested in Honey having puppies?' I said a bit snappily.

'Of course I'm interested!' Molly said, looking a bit hurt. 'Why wouldn't I be?'

'I thought that Puppy Power was the best thing since sliced toast and that you didn't need real dogs who were difficult to wash and had to be taken for real long walks,' I muttered.

Molly went reddish and almost looked ashamed of herself for a moment. 'I didn't say that!' she protested.

'Well, you have certainly been vastly more

interested in that computer game than in my puppy-related problems,' I mumbled.

Molly looked at the floor.

'In fact,' I went on, Warming to my Theme, 'I had to give up on you when it came to Masterly Plans, and if it hadn't been for Frank and the DVD, Mum would never have changed her mind.'

Molly looked up at me in total and utter **shock** and opened her mouth to protest again. But then she shut it and sighed. 'I'm sorry,' she said. 'You're right.'

Now it was my turn to look shocked. Molly never said anyone else was right!

'The thing is,' she said sheepishly, 'I've sort of been a bit jealous of you lately. I mean, I know we won the Talent Contest together in the end and everything, but Honey is actually really *your* dog, and you get to have her at your house all the time. I'm not allowed a

133

dog — you know that. That's why my auntie gave me Puppy Power in the end. Mum apparently told her she thought it would stop me nagging her and Dad for a real dog.'

'And has it?' I asked, suddenly feeling really quite guilty. I had been spending so much time feeling sorry for myself that I hadn't even noticed that my Bestest Friend in the entire universe had been pining after a pooch of her very own.

'No,' said Molly simply. 'I mean, the game is fun and everything, but you can't cuddle a piece of plastic, can you?'

I giggled a bit when she said this, as it made me think of Molly trying to snuggle up to her computer game or trying to take it out for a walk

on the lead and it did seem quite a hilarious
image.

We had a celebratory Best Friend hug
and I promised to let Molly help in all things
puppy-related from now on, and she promised
not to go on and on about Puppy Power
too much any more. Then Mum came in
and we turned our attention to the food and
DEMOLISHED it all, which means we gobbled
our breakfast right down to the last crumb.

'By the way, Nick's coming with us to the
breeder's,' Mum said as we cleared the table.

'Hurrah!' I shouted.

'Oooh!' said Molly, clasping her hands and
scrunching up her face and shoulders in an
all-over-body expression of excitableness. 'I so
can't wait for Honey to have puppies!'

Mum smiled and said, 'Well, you'll have
to, young lady! Come on – I think I heard
Nick's car. And be quiet – we don't want April

135

to break the habit of a lifetime and get up early. She might spot her ex-boyfriend waiting outside, and then we'll have World War Three on our hands.'

I agreed with Mum. When we had told April the night before that we were going to see a breeder, April had just yawned and said, 'Do I look interested?' So hopefully this meant that she would not be getting up any time soon.

We went out with Honey to meet Nick.

'Hi! All set?' was all he said.

He didn't look as excited as I personally thought he should have done, considering how marvellously magnificent it was that we were finally going to the breeder. In fact he looked a bit uncomfortable, like he had just smelt a pongy whiff or something. And he kept checking over his shoulder.

We were going in Nick's car as he had

met the breeder before and knew the way to
his house.

Honey was going to have to sit in the back
with me and Molly, as Nick did not have a
very big car. She wasn't very keen on that idea.

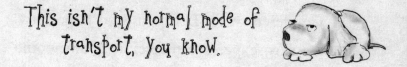

This isn't my normal mode of
transport, you know.

'You are still a bouncy girl, aren't you?' said
Nick, turning round and rubbing her head.
'Poor old Honey – you don't know what's
about to hit you, do you? You won't be
bouncing about like this for a while.'

'What do you mean?' I asked.

'Being pregnant is quite tiring for the mum,
you know,' Nick explained, starting the engine.

I'm always full of Beans! And
sausages . . .

'How come?' Molly asked.

Nick smiled. 'Honey's body will have to work hard to give her puppies all the nutrients they need while they are growing. She'll be very sleepy and you'll need to give her lots of TLC.'

I wondered what TLC was and hoped it wasn't a very expensive medicine. Mum would freak if she thought we'd have to spend a lot of money.

Mum sighed and said to Nick, 'You know, sometimes I wonder how Honey will be as a mum. I mean, she's still a puppy herself really. What is she going to be like when she's got six or eight babies to look after?'

'Don't worry. Honey will know what to do,' Nick said.

We pooches are generally quite perfect.

How to Choose Your Breeder

'What other things will happen to Honey once she's expecting?' I asked.

'Well, she might go off her food a bit,' Nick said.

Molly started rummaging in her pink bag with the purple flowers on, which she liked to carry around with her at that time.

'Hold on a sec,' she said. 'I've brought a new notebook along so that we can keep track of all the things we need to know. Ah, there we are – go on, Nick. Give us some veterinary-type details of the Puppy Producing Procedure.'

Nick laughed. 'You are organized,' he said. 'Actually, it's a good idea to keep a notebook or a diary of Honey's pregnancy. OK – so what else do you want to know?'

'Erm, how long do we have to wait for the pups to be born?' I asked.

'Well,' said Nick, 'once Honey has mated you need to count ahead nine weeks, or sixty-four days actually, to get the date that the pups will hopefully be born.'

As Molly scribbled away I was busily counting ahead on my fingers, which was quite difficult as I kept losing track, but eventually I said, 'Oh my heavens above! I have just worked out that if everything goes according to plan, Honey will have her pups—'

'—around Christmas time,' Mum finished. 'Well, that would make it a special holiday wouldn't it?'

Molly had stopped scribbling and gone unusually quiet. I wondered if she was already making a Masterly Plan to ask her Mum for an extra-special Christmas present.

Honey sighed a loud and grunty doggy-sigh and flopped on the floor of the car.

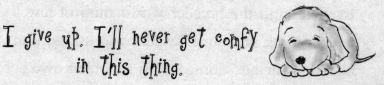

I give up. I'll never get comfy in this thing.

'Hang on a minute,' said Mum. 'I don't want to be boring, but we're jumping the gun a bit here, aren't we? There's no telling when – or if – Honey will become pregnant. Let's just see how today goes.'

I must admit I was not that chuffed about the breeder when we first saw him. He looked a bit like a grown-up version of Mr Frank Stink-i-verse Gritter – in other words, dirty and grimy. And his house was rather messy too, but it was so full of dogs that luckily I got distractivated quite quickly from the pongs.

This place is heaven!

Even though the breeder was a man of few
words, Nick was super-brilliant at asking him
all the right questions. Molly scribbled away
the whole time, taking notes on everything.
Mum found the whole thing RIVETING,
which means that she was glued to every
word – in other words, fascinated.

Me too! I could stay
here forever!

At long last the grown-ups said we could take
Honey to see the kennels.

There were four very huge outdoor kennels,
which were really just like cages, and only two
of them had dogs in.

'The stud dogs are round the back, out of
the way – we'll see them in a mo. The mothers
and the new litters are here where it's quieter,'
Nick said, pointing at the nearest cages. 'They

have to stay enclosed,' he went on. 'Pups aren't allowed out until they've been weaned and had all their jabs.'

I felt actually very proud as I knew all this already. 'Yes, I remember that from when we first had Honey,' I said. 'She had to come off her mum's milk first and be weaned on to real dog food, and then she had injections to stop her getting diseases.'

We went right up to the cage. I could not believe my eyes when I saw how tiny some of the pups were.

'They are titchical!' I squealed. 'How old are those ones?' I pointed to the kennel on the left, where there was literally a pile of pups heaped one on top of the other, all snoozing next to their mum, who looked totally exhaustified by the whole thing. Honey strained on her lead to get close to the cage.

Let me say 'hi'!

Nick took Honey's lead from me. 'I'll hold on to Honey so you can take a closer look,' he said. 'I tell you what — is it OK if I take her to meet the stud dogs?'

'Sure,' I said.

'Do you want to come with us, Angela?' Nick asked her. 'Or do you want to hold one of the new pups?'

Mum's face said the answer before her mouth did. She was fixated on the heap of squidgy puppies and had got that crumply, soppy look that she had when she first saw Honey.

'I guess that's a done deal then!' Nick laughed. 'Honey, you're coming with me.'

Awww! Do I have to?

How to Choose Your Breeder

Mum, Molly and I each picked up a puppy. The breeder had said they were only two weeks' old, so they were exactly the same age as Honey had been the first time I had laid my eyes on her. 'Can you believe that Honey was once this size?' I asked Mum.

She shook her head but didn't say anything. Oh no! She had gone all teary again!

'You babies grow up so quickly,' she said quietly as she stroked the teeny creature in her hand.

145

Puppy Power

I looked at Molly and rolled my eyes, but Molly hissed, 'Don't say anything! She is soooo On Side! She couldn't be *more* On Side – unless you waved a red card at her and blew a whistle in her face.'

What on earth was Molly talking about red cards and whistles for? I wondered vaguely. However, she was right about one thing: there was no chance Mum would say 'no' now.

She was hooked.

12
How to Go into Planning Mode

On the way home, Mum, Molly and I could not stop nattering about how we were going to plan for the pups' arrival. Nick said that Honey seemed to get on especially well with one of the male dogs called Poplar.

'I must admit I preferred Poplar to the other dog too,' he went on. 'The other one was really bouncy, but Poplar was more relaxed and cuddly.'

'Is that important?' Molly asked, scribbling away again.

'Oh yes,' said Nick. 'You have to know the

147

dad's character as well as the mum's, because it gives you some idea about the kind of pups you'll be getting. You don't want aggressive or over-energetic pups, believe me!'

Mum laughed. 'Yes – Honey's bouncy enough on her own!'

Nothing Wrong With a Bit of Bounce.

Poplar was a black Labrador who had already been a dad a few times. The breeder had been very proud of him and said he came from a good pedigree. He had shown Nick all the paperwork, and Nick was happy for Honey to stay with Poplar in a couple of weeks' time.

'A couple of weeks' time!' I had groaned. 'Why not now?'

How to Go into Planning Mode

It was going to take *nine weeks* for the puppies to grow inside her as it was — why did we have to wait two more until Honey could stay with Poplar?

Mum and Nick looked at each other.

'Honey's not ready yet,' Nick said simply. And that was that.

At last, after two weeks of **Hell** at school with Mrs Wotherspoon throwing herself at me like a whole ton of bricks for every single thing I did (and didn't do), and two weeks of crossing the days off the calendar, Honey went to stay with Poplar. She was only gone for a couple of days, but the house felt very empty and strange without her around. When we got her back again, Nick told us in a most cryptical way that everything had 'gone very well' and that we should generally Keep An Eye on Honey and tell him if we noticed Anything Unusual.

Whatever that meant. Nick promised that he would be On Hand for us and that I could call him whenever I wanted.

And so Molly and I went into Planning for Puppies Mode.

And I went into Planning for Snooze Mode.

Frank also came round to see how Things Had Gone. Mum thought it was 'sweet' that Frank wanted to get involved, which slightly set my teeth on their edges, but I was so grateful to him for finding a way to get Mum to change her mind that I didn't really mind him being there.

We left Honey to relax in her basket and took some drinks and snacks into the Den so that we could start our Planning Session.

Frank was being quite a laugh and kept saying things like, 'Do you think Honey and

Poplar are in luuuuuuurve like Romeo and Juliet?'

Honey 4 Poplar

HP

Then he put on a dramatical over-the-top Shakespeare accent and said, 'Honey-o, Honey-o, wherefore art thou, Honey-o?'

I'm snoozing in my Bed-i-o.

Molly, however, did not find it one iota of a fraction amusing.

'Frank,' she said, 'instead of acting like the fool that you are, could you please go away and leave us in peace?'

'OOOOOOOH!' Frank replied. 'Well,
if that's your attitude—'

'STOP!' I yelled at the pair of them.
'Listen, Frank, instead of arguing with Molly,
why don't you give me some *proper advice* on
how to get ready for the pups' arrival?'

Molly did her sh_ocked and surprised
face when I said this, which nearly almost
made her choke as she was crunching on a
mouthful of double-choc-chip cookie at the
time.

'No Way Ho-Zay!' she shouted, her eyes
all big and round like they were going to pop
out of their sockets right there and then. 'We
didn't need HIS help last time with Honey, so
I don't see one little bit why we need HIS help
now.'

I gave Molly a long look to show her that
she did not know what she was talking about.
'Molly,' I said slowly, 'getting one eight-

week-old puppy and bringing it home is quite
a different matter from having *seven or eight
newborn* pups to look after.'

'But Honey will do most of the looking
after, won't she?' Molly asked, a bit puzzled.

'She will to start with, but she will need lots
of help, Nick said,' I explained.

'Yeah,' said Frank, grinning his head off.
'And the thing is, Miss Know-It-All Molly Cook,
my dog Meatball has actually *had* puppies, and *I*
was there, so *I* know all about it.'

'He's right,' I said, not letting Molly's
SCARY AND FLARY look put me off
for once.

Molly frowned and did a grimacey thing
with her mouth. 'All right,' she said when she
saw that I had no Intention of Backing Down.
'Please could you after all give us some advice,
Frank?' she asked, not looking at him as she
spoke.

Puppy Power

'What's it worth?' Frank asked, picking his nose in the most unattractive way possible by scraping his finger round and round his nostril to get the hugest and stickiest bogey he could find. He eventually extractivated it and examined it close up. Goodness knows what he thought he would find in it – the Crown Jewels?

'Listen, there is no need to be disgustivating,' I said, becoming quite severely stern. 'And anyway, if you really want to know what it is worth, I think it is worth you not flicking that bogey at us,' I said firmly.

'Don't worry, I wouldn't waste it on you,' said Frank, popping it into his actual mouth right in front of us! Honestly, just as I think I can bear his company, he goes and ruins it by being Mr Gross-o-vator.

I took a deep breath and ignored his grim and inhuman behaviour. 'What do

How to Go into Planning Mode

we need to do first, Frank?' I asked.

'Let's see – first of all you need a notebook to record all the important dates and things,' he said.

'Check!' said Molly, waving her pink notebook at him in a very pleased-with-herself way.

'Then you must make a list of everything you'll need for the birth and *then*, you have to note down everything about the dog during the pregnancy – her weight and stuff – and *then*, when the pups are born, there is loads of information that you have to keep track of, like how much each pup weighs and so on.'

This was absolutely the Way To Molly's Heart as she is the *Queen of Lists*.

'Sounds dudey,' said Molly. 'What else?'

'Then you need to prepare a den to put the whelping bed in,' he said.

'Whoooa!' said Molly. 'Stop right there. What's a whelping bed? It sounds like an instrument of torture.'

Frank and I rolled our eyes at each other. 'The whelping bed is the bed the puppies are born in and where they spend the first few weeks of their life,' I said.

'Oh *that* – I knew that,' said Molly.

Frank spluttered a bit with laughter, but Pulled Himself Together when he caught sight of Molly's glare and told us that we would also need a thermometer and lots of newspapers.

'Then you must make a list and go shopping for the things you'll need,' he added.

I was secretly vastly impressed with that. Surely even Molly would agree that a boy who suggests a shopping trip is a pretty amazing sort of person.

'Hurrah!' I said.

156

How to Go into Planning Mode

'Yahooo!' said Molly. 'Shopping! It'll be a faberoony way to pass the time and stop us from going bonkers-crazy with Excitement!'

We had just over half a term to get ready. A whole nine weeks. How would we cope? And it was coming up to Christmas too. How much could the human brain deal with before it simply popped with an overload of ultra-excitable activity, I wondered?

By the end of the first week alone we had made a Comprehensive List of What to Have to Hand for the Big Event:

- Clean towels
- Fresh bedding (e.g. old newspapers)
- New notebook and pen for timing births and events leading to births

- Formula newborn-puppy milk
  (in case of feeding problems)
- Small feeding bottle
  (also in case of problems)
- Emergency telephone number
  for vet

'Hey, listen to this!' Molly said one Friday night when she was sleeping over. 'You know Nick said he would have to check Honey at twenty-one-ish days to see how she was getting on? Well, in Monica Sitstill's book it says that by then he will be able to FEEL THE PUPPIES!'

'Show me!' I cried, scrabbling to get a closer look.

> At about five weeks it is possible to feel the fetuses. Your vet will gently prod the mother's belly to see how many puppies there are.

Oh. My. Goodness.

I was actually getting too excited to breathe, just thinking about Nick feeling lots of tiny pups inside Honey's tummy! It was a bit science-fictiony and **freaky**, but mega-exciting at the same time!

How was I going to wait until Day 21?

159

13
How to Cook a Dog's Dinner

As it turned out, Mrs Wotherspoon kept us busy with extra homework and practices for the Christmas play (which, thank the high heavens, was NOT *Romeo and Juliet*, or anything else Shakespearical or romantic-ish) and so the first month went more quickly than I had thought it would.

Also I was distractivated by Honey, whose behaviour was not entirely what I would describe as 'normal' in an everyday kind of fashion.

Me? I'm totally normal . . .

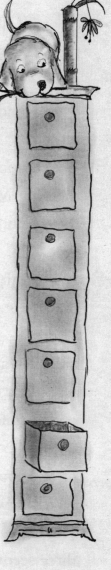

For a start, she slept so much
that I thought she might
actually be competing for
a gold medal in the Sleep Olympics.

'Poor little Honey,' Mum kept
saying while she patted her on the
head and scratched under her chin.
'It's tiring when you're expecting,
isn't it, Poochy?'

I am a little weary, yes . . .

Mum had gone really
DOOLALLY-BANANAS in
her fussing over Honey. But when
I said something to this effect,

she said, 'I've been a mum twice you know –' Er, yes, I did know that actually, thanks Mum for treating me like a complete Fruit Loop. '– so I understand how Honey's feeling, that's all.'

Hmmm. I was not one bit sure that I liked the way Mum was Bonding with Honey over this Mummy Thing.

We mums understand one another!

Still, it was important to keep Mum On Side, especially as Honey's behaviour weirded me out at times.

For example, one morning I put her bowl of dog food down and said, 'Sit,' and, 'Wait,' which is what I always do before I allow Honey to dive in and scoff the lot in her usual three seconds flat. (This is a ROUTINE that

How to Cook a Dog's Dinner

Honey and I had got into ever since she was a puppy.) Anyway, when I was ready for her to eat, I said, 'Go on!' as normal.

Nothing happened.

'Go on, Honey!' I said in a reassuringly kind manner. 'It's your breakfast.'

Honey just flopped down in a droopy sad way and sighed heavily.

I really can't face that gross Brown stuff today.

'Oh, Honey – you've gone off your food!' I said. This had never happened before. I supposed it was because of being pregnant, but nevertheless a tiny bit of me was feeling really quite worried that there might in fact be something disastrously wrong with her.

I tried tempting Honey with a bit of food

163

in my hand. 'Come on, Honey-Bun. Come and taste the lovely yummy food.'

Nothing. She just sat and stared at me.

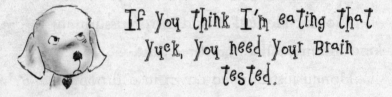

If you think I'm eating that Yuck, you need Your Brain tested.

After about half an hour of trying to get Honey to eat (I even tried to feed her by hand) I gave up and went to make myself some toast.

Just as it was beginning to smell particularly yummy, Honey heaved herself up from her floppy position on the floor and came and nudged me with her nose.

Now THAT is a tasty smell!

'Do you want some?' I asked.

That's the general idea.

I took the toast from the toaster and broke off a corner to let it cool while I spread some peanut butter on the rest of the slice for me. Then I picked up the corner of toast and bent down to give it to Honey. She gobbled it up and licked her lips and then nudged me again. Oh well, dogs eat anything usually, I thought. Maybe Honey would like peanut butter. I held out the rest of the slice and told Honey to sit just like before. She sat immediately and looked at the peanut-buttery toast in a particularly **BEADY-EYED** fashion. And then she started drooling!

'Funny pooch!' I said and gave her the toast. She swallowed it in one mouthful, so I quickly made another slice for her.

That is the most delicious snack I have ever had!

After we had both finished off a few more slices, I went to have a look in my very own personal copy of *Perfect Puppies* to see if there was anything to explain this bizarreness.

> Often a dog will go off her usual diet in the early stages of pregnancy. This is perfectly normal. She may also develop particular cravings. For example, some dogs will only eat chicken and rice, some scrambled eggs.

'What's this?' Mum said that evening, coming into the kitchen to find me cooking. 'Are you in trouble at school or something?'

'No. Why?' I asked. Mum does often put two and two together and get one hundred and fifty-six. Why would me cooking some eggs mean that I was in trouble at school?

166

How to Cook a Dog's Dinner

'It's just, I've never seen you cook anything that doesn't have chocolate in it,' Mum said, laughing, 'and you've definitely never cooked your own tea before, so I wondered if you were trying to prepare me for some bad news.'

Ah. Mum thought I was cooking *my* tea. Whoops.

'Er, the thing is, Mum. I'm not actually cooking these eggs for me. I would happily cook my own tea, but I've just used all the eggs I could find,' I added hastily, seeing her frown.

'Who exactly *are* you cooking them for then? Oh . . .'

Honey was sitting at my feet and looking up at me in a distinctly expectifying way.

 I'm looking forward to this!

'Don't get cross!' I cried as Mum's frown went darker and more dangerous-looking. 'Honey hasn't eaten any of her own food and I was starting to get worried, so I checked in *Perfect Puppies* and Monica Sitstill says it's very important to realize that dogs sometimes get a bit fussy when they are expecting—'

'A BIT fussy?' Mum exclaimed in a quite over-the-top fashion. 'Since when do dogs eat butter and CREAM in their scrambled eggs?

How to Cook a Dog's Dinner

I've heard of cravings, but this is ridiculous. Even *I* wasn't this expensive to feed when I was expecting!'

'Mum,' I pleaded, 'will you stop going on about you being pregnant? It's kind of embarrassing.'

Mum crossed her arms and raised her eyebrows. 'Humph,' she said. 'I think after this little *Mastercook* episode I'm entitled to say what I like!' But her mouth twitched into a bit of a smile as she was saying this. 'It's all right,' she said, rolling her eyes a bit. 'I know that Madam here needs special treatment. Just make sure you ask me before you go using all the nice food. And for goodness sake, use milk next time instead of cream!'

Honey's eating habits were not the only weird–doolally thing that happened to her in the early weeks. She also started paying a lot more attention to our cats, Cheese and Toast, than she had ever paid before – even in the early days when she had tried to get them to play puppy games with her. She kept moping over to them when they were sleeping, and nuzzling them.

These little guys need a mama.

She tried washing them, and once she even tried to pick Toast up in her mouth by the scruff of his neck!

Come to Mummy, my little baby!

Needless to say, Cheese and Toast were not having any of it.

What's up with these little puppies?

How to Cook a Dog's Dinner

It actually was quite hilariously amusing
to watch, even if poor Honey ended
up getting her nose scratched a few
too many times. In the end I thought
it was kinder to encourage her to have one
of my old cuddly toys to 'look after'. I chose
a toy monkey, which was more 'manky' than
'monkey', as it had been sucked and chewed
by me when I was a baby, but Honey loved
it and looked after it tenderly as if it
was her own little one.

She had always been quite a loop-the-loop
crazy
bonkers dog, but thinking a chewed old
monkey toy was her own real puppy . . . that
was taking her doolaliness to a whole new
level.

Isn't my baby adorable?

14

How to Nearly Die from Anticipation

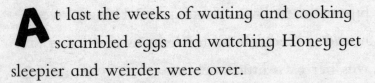

At last the weeks of waiting and cooking scrambled eggs and watching Honey get sleepier and weirder were over.

'Can I ring Nick?' I asked Mum. 'Purleeeeeeeeeese!'

'Yes, I think we need him to check up on our little poochie, don't we?' Mum said, fussing over Honey, who was washing Manky-Monkey-Baby with extra-special tenderness.

'It's Day 21!' I announced as soon as Nick came on the line.

'Come to the surgery this evening,' he said.

How to Nearly Die from Anticipation

'Oh, OK,' I said, feeling a bit puzzled. 'But I thought you said you'd come round here so that Honey didn't get anxious—'

'I would prefer it if you came here,' he said quickly.

He sounded quite definite, so I said, 'OK. Can't wait! See you then.'

That evening Mum drove us to the surgery. We picked up Molly on the way, as I didn't think it would be fair to leave her out of this mega-important event. We were so excited that we couldn't speak. We just squealed a lot instead, which is what we do when our tummies are so squirmy with ANTICIPATION (in other words, looking-forwardness) that we cannot think of any words that will describe the feeling. Honey, on the other hand, just slumped in the boot of the car and whined a bit.

173

I was TRYING to snooze . . .

We got to the vet's nice and early. As
Mum parked the car I had a sudden
HORRENDOUS thought which stopped
me mid-squeal.

'What's up?' Molly asked, noticing the look
of Utmost Horror on my face (eyes wide open,
jaw gaping, eyebrows shooting their way up to
the stars).

'We're going to have to talk to the Bottom
Shuffler A.K.A. the Scarlet Woman,' I hissed.

'Who's the Bottom Shuffler?' Mum asked.

'She's the nurse that looks like April,' I said.
'You know – the one April is humongously
jealous of and thinks that Nick is going out
with.'

Mum just sighed and said, 'Come on,
Honey,' carefully helping her out of the boot.

How to Nearly Die from Anticipation

We followed Mum into the reception area. Thank the high heavens above, the Bottom Shuffler wasn't there. Nick was.

'Hello! I thought you'd be early,' he said, grinning. 'And luckily for you, my last patient has not turned up, so I can see you right away. Oh, Honey looks a bit dopey, doesn't she?' he added.

What are we doing in this place?

'So, er, Nick – where's the Bottom Shuffler?' Molly asked. I nearly almost hit her in actual public.

'Who?' said Nick, looking quite perplexed.

'Oh, no one,' I said quickly, and jabbed Molly in the ribs as SUBTLY as I could. 'Shouldn't we get on with the Matter in Hand, which is, of course, Honey?' I asked, trying to Move Events Swiftly On.

175

We followed Nick into his room. He bent down and tickled Honey's tummy, feeling it very gently. 'There, there, Honey,' he said, 'I'm just going to give you a bit of a tickle . . .'

Why didn't you say so? I LOVE tummy-tickles.

I was standing beside myself with the amount of nervousness I was feeling.

'Don't press too hard, will you?' I said. I straight away realized that was a stupid and embarrassing thing to say to a vet who obviously Knows What He Is Doing. But on the other hand, you can never be too careful, and Honey was my One and Only Bestest Pooch in the whole entire world, which meant that her puppies were the Bestest Puppies in the whole entire world too, and I couldn't bear the thought that anyone might hurt them.

Nick smiled reassuringly and, taking his stethoscope, said, 'I promise I won't.'

All of a sudden I felt so lucky to have a vet who was someone I knew and could trust, and I realized that I had really missed having Nick around in a Non-Professional Capacity. I wished April and he would get back together so that he would want to come round to our

177

house again. I felt a bit EMOTIONAL – in other words, as if my eyes might go leaky. I squeezed them shut, just in case.

Nick helped Honey up on to her feet and stood behind her, then very gently he squeezed her tummy around a bit. When he had finished his examination he had a very serious expression on his face, and for one split of a moment I was extremely anxious.

But then his face opened out into such a huge *beamy* smile that it could only mean one thing:

'I am delighted to say that I can feel at least seven puppies!' he said.

'SEVEN!' I yelled. And Molly and even Mum whooped with excitement and joy.

Seven cute, tiny puppies! I was in heaven just thinking about it. I flung my arms around Mum and then Molly and then we all hugged Honey.

What's all the fuss about?

'You are a superstar, Honey!' I mumbled into Honey's silky fur.

Don't I know it!

'She may need a little bit more food from now on,' said Nick, 'because her body is working very hard to give the puppies everything they need to grow big and strong inside her.'

I didn't think Honey would have any complaints about that! But when I looked at her she looked too sleepy to want to even bother with eating. Poor Poochy.

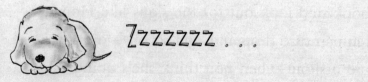

Zzzzzzz . . .

Nick went on. 'But that doesn't mean you

should overfeed her. Indigestion can be a problem in pregnancy—'

'Tell me about it!' Mum said grimly.

Oh no! I did not want her Going Off On One about her own pregnancies in front of Nick. I coughed loudly and Nick smiled and patted my snoozing dog on the head.

'Well, Summer, all we've got to do now is wait until D-Day!'

'What is D-Day?' I asked, looking a bit worried.

'Delivery Day!' Nick said. 'Remember the timetable you drew up to plan when the puppies would be due? Well, about six weeks from now Honey will be ready to deliver her pups. Keep reading your *Perfect Puppies* book and look out for the signs like Honey's temperature dropping and so on – and give me a shout when you think she's going into labour.'

How to Nearly Die from Anticipation

Mum looked at him sharply. 'Why? Are you going to come round and help? I thought you didn't want to—'

'Of course,' Nick said. 'I wouldn't miss seeing Honey's pups being born for anything . . .' He tailed off and shuffled his feet a bit. 'That's if it's OK with you, Angela.'

Mum looked OVERJOYED with relief. 'Yes, please!' she said.

I thought even Honey smiled in her sleep.

Molly and I just about managed to survive until the bell rang on the last day of term, even though all that waiting was AGONY with a capital A . . .

But at last D-Day was around the corner! It was also going to be Christmas Day, but that was not in the front of my mind at all (for the first time in my life) because of the puppies. If someone had asked me the year before if I would ever not be excited about Christmas Day and all the presents and things, I would have said, 'Are you bonkers round-the-bend? Christmas is the most thrilling thing that ever happens in my life!'

But this time it was not true, and I could not have cared less about a fat man dressed in red and white trying to climb down chimneys at midnight.

The most wondrous thing that had made me OVER THE TOP OF THE MOON with looking-forwardness was that for a while I had actually seen the puppies moving around inside Honey's tummy.

How to Nearly Die from Anticipation

I obviously do not mean that I had actual real X-ray vision – it was just that the puppies had got so big inside Honey that instead of her tummy looking quite wobbly and fat –

Excuse me! Who are you calling fat?

– you could see little lumps and bumps moving under the surface of her fur. Poor Honey – it must have been very uncomfortable. Mum seemed to get quite distressed about it too: you would have thought that *she* was having puppies herself!

'Oh, Honey darling!' she would say. 'You must be so tired out. I think you should sit with her and stroke her to make her feel loved, Summer.'

Just what I was thinking.

And she also kept on saying things which
FREAKED me out, like, 'I remember giving
birth to you and April like it was yesterday.
Goodness me, I couldn't wait to get you out
towards the end.'

'MUM! FOR THE LAST TIME – STOP
IT!'

I could tell that actually if Honey had been
able to speak, she and Mum would have had
lots of conversations agreeing with each other.
My beloved pooch looked so woebegone most
of the time.

Something's doing cartwheels inside
me – of course I'm woebegone!

Meanwhile, Molly and I had decided to take
it in turns to Keep Watch. One of the most
important things we had to do was to take
Honey's temperature every hour.

184

How to Nearly Die from Anticipation

This is what *Perfect Puppies* had to say:

> The first signs that your dog is about to 'whelp',
> or give birth, are restlessness and panting. It is
> important to take her temperature often. It will
> fall from 38.6 °C to around 36.7 °C just before
> she starts to whelp.

Molly and I knew the section 'What to
Expect When Your Pup is Expecting' almost
completely off by heart, and we knew that the
dog knows just by nature exactly what to do
and doesn't need the help of a human or even
a vet to give birth.

'Don't you think that's astoundingly
amazing?' Molly said.

'What do you mean?' I asked, scribbling
furious notes in my notebook. (I had one of my
own now – I was not going to let Molly be the
only one to have a special Puppy Notebook
when it was my actual dog having a litter.)

'I mean,' said Molly impatiently, 'imagine

185

if *humans* were born knowing how to do their seven times table just by *natural instinct*? Imagine just having the Knack of speaking in French or German or Spanish at the flick of a finger without having to actually learn it?'

'Yes!' I said, getting into the Swing Of Things. 'And imagine being able to make lemon meringue pie standing on your head . . .'

I don't know where this random-ish comment had come from. I don't even like lemon meringue pie, and I didn't obviously mean that you would be literally standing on your head, of course – if you could do that it would be probably quite a good

circus act, I suppose, but it wouldn't really be that useful because all the lemony bits and meringue would just fall on top of you because of gravitational forces – unless you lived on the moon, in which case it would just float everywhere and you wouldn't be able to eat it anyway. Everyone knows they don't eat lemon meringue pie in outermost space.

Molly looked at me weirdly and said, 'Yes, so anyway . . . isn't Honey clever to know just what to do?'

She was indeed a very clever pooch and as her owner it made me feel very proud inside, which was like a **fizzy** feeling that was warm and nice at the same time.

'Honey, you are a marvel!' I told her.

That's me!

Mum had said Molly was welcome round

at ours any time she liked now it was the
holidays, and so of course that meant that
she had practically moved in for the whole of
Week Nine. We simply did not want to miss a
single second of being with Honey in case D-
Day came early. We spent most of that week
getting her den ready.

> The whelping box should be a large drawer-like
> box, lined with plenty of newspaper. It should
> be possible for the mother to get in and out, but
> not the puppies.

'We need to find a room where we can keep
Honey quiet and also where people won't be
constantly coming in and disturbing her,' Molly
said as we got all the newspapers I'd been saving
and the cardboard box for the puppies' bed.

'I know – I've thought of that. Follow me,'
I said, walking into the back room, which had
all the GUBBINS – in other words, stuff, in it.
'I thought this would be a great place. Honey

188

How to Nearly Die from Anticipation

sleeps in this room most of the time anyway, as there's only the washing machine and boring things like that in here. No one ever comes in.'

'Excuse *me*, young lady!' Mum said, staggering through the door with a mountain of ironing and nearly tripping over our newspaper pile. 'NOBODY comes in here? Who do you think does the laundry in this house?'

I sighed heavily and rolled my eyes right up into the back of my head to show how exasperational Mum could be sometimes. 'Obviously *you* do, Mum,' I said in an over-the-top patient sort of manner. 'What I meant was, no one *else* does.'

'Tell me about it,' Mum muttered, plonking down the ironing and storming out again, mumbling to herself.

Molly and I decided to ignore Mum's IRRATIONAL behaviour – in other words, her bizarreness – and set to work putting the cardboard box in the corner of the room.

When it was ready Molly said, 'Let's get Honey in here to try it out.'

I fetched my big heavy pooch from where she was snoozing by the radiator in the kitchen. She had taken to lying there recently, and I didn't blame her as it was certainly **Freezing McSneezing** now that it was nearly Christmas and the days were so dark and gloomy.

'Come on, Honey-Bun. Come and see your lovely whelping box,' I said in a soothing way.

I was having such a nice dream about sausages . . .

Honey waddled over to the cardboard box and plonked

herself heavily on to the newspapers. And closed her eyes.

Now, where was I?

Molly laughed. 'Honey seems right at home already.'

It was fantabulous, I thought. Everything had gone really well with our preparations and we had had no worries about Honey's pregnancy.

Personally the only problematical thing that I could imagine happening was April seeing Nick, which was obviously going to happen when he came to help with the births.

Then I suddenly remembered what Mum had said about making 'someone else's dreams come true'.

Was this all part of a Molly-style Masterly Plan cooked up by Mum to get Nick and April back together?

191

15
How to Go Doolally with Excitement

By Christmas Eve Molly and I were starting to get a bit jittery – in other words, we were beside ourselves with nerves and panic. It was Day 63, which meant the next day was D-Day!

'What shall we do, Molls?' I asked. 'We can't sit here looking at Honey all day.'

'Let's do some Christmas decorations,' Molly suggested. 'This place doesn't look very Festive, does it?'

I agreed. 'Mum's been too busy

working cos she's taking extra holiday when
the pups arrive,' I explained. We had a
Christmas tree in the sitting room,
but that was it.

So we set to, distractivating

 ourselves, using tinsel and sparkly
things that we found in a box
in the cupboard on the landing.

Unfortunately it didn't take long to
finish the decorations, as my house is not
very big. So we were soon back in the
kitchen at Honey's side, watching her
every breath with worry and concern.
I didn't want to leave her for a second,
but it soon became obvious that I was
going to have to, if I needed the loo, for
example.

I wish you WOULD leave
me alone.

Molly was anxious that she was not going to be allowed to stay, as her parents were having a party that evening.

'Mum always asks a couple of random-ish aunts and some neighbours,' Molly said, curling her lip in a most disapproving manner. 'It's deadly dull and yawnsome and I have to be polite and answer questions about school even though it's the holidays!'

I agreed that it was mega-unfair. 'But surely she will make an Exception for Honey's Big Day?' I asked.

'She'd better!' Molly said, making her face look quite scarily THREATENING in nature. I would have given in to her if I was her mum, that's for sure.

Me too!

While we were trying to think of a way to get

How to Go Doolally with Excitement

Mrs Cook to let Molly stay with us for another day (and possibly a night!) Mum staggered into the kitchen looking severely UNSIGH₹LY.

'You two have been making a lot of noise—' she said blearily. 'Oh! I love the decorations! . . . But . . . where's Honey?' she added, looking round the room.

Honey had gone from her basket!

'Oh!' I cried. 'She was with us a second ago.'

We all rushed around a bit madly, looking for her. I hoped she hadn't run away. I had read in *Perfect Puppies* that dogs in the wild will try to find a quiet spot away from the rest of the pack to have their litters. Maybe Honey had left the house to get away from us?

'It's OK, she's taken up RESIDENCE in her den,' Molly said importantly, coming out of the back room. 'In other words, she has moved

195

in there, which I think must be A Sign that something is definitely happening.'

'Oh. My. Goodness!' I cried, and rushed in to check on her. She had been pacing up and down but was now very quietly lying in the whelping box. I bent down to look at her.

'Do you think she's panting?' I asked Molly worriedly, checking again in *Perfect Puppies* for 'Signs That Your Dog May Be Going into Whelp'. 'I am not at all sure that her breathing is in any way normal.'

Molly bent closer to Honey to listen carefully. 'I think she's just snoring,' she said.

I was sleeping, until you stuck your shout in my face!

Mum stirred her tea with a biro, which she then stuck behind her ear. 'I think we should call Nick and ask him to come over,' she

How to Go Doolally with Excitement

said in a vague and distractivated manner, pouring the tea on to her toast.

I nodded enthusiastically. 'And Frank too,' I said.

Molly started to breathe in deeply as if she was going to say something that would vastly contradiction what I had just suggested, so I quickly added, 'Remember, Frank's been through this all before with Meatball, so he'll know if Honey is ready for the Whelping and Giving Birth MALARKY or whether she is just in fact snoring.'

Mum pointed the dripping-wet biro at me.

'You call Frank and I'll call Nick,' she said, sounding like a policewoman in a highly Tense and Critical telly-type drama.

'Don't do that,' said a quiet voice.

'April!' said Mum, jumping so high in the air she nearly smashed the dangly-down light that hung from the ceiling. 'You're up early.'

'Yes,' said April simply. 'I couldn't sleep.'

'Oh dear,' said Mum.

No one could think of anything else to say. Except Molly.

'Is it because you are worried about Nick and the Bottom Shuffler?' she asked. Mum and I glared hard at Molly, but she continued. 'Cos if it is, you are being a bit silly, if you ask me. I mean, I've only heard about this woman from Summer, but she sounds like a Right Nightmare. Why would Nick want to go out with a Right Nightmare when he's got a lovely girlfriend like you?'

How to Go Doolally with Excitement

What was Molly doing? I thought, the nerves and panic I was already feeling rising like a SICK SENSATION in my throat. 'I bet if you had a Sane and Sensible conversation with him, you would discover that it is all In Your Mind and that Nick still loves you just as much as you love him,' she went on, ignoring me staring at her so hard my eyeballs were beginning to hurt. 'In fact, why don't you call him now and use Honey as an excuse to get him round here, and then we'll give you some Space to sort it all out?'

Where in all the earth did Molly learn how to be so psychiatrical about other people's relationships? I wondered. I could not imagine that April would in any way appreciate being told how to solve her *Love-Life Problems* by a ten-year-old. I glanced quickly at April and winced a bit as I waited for the Inevitable Explosion . . .

199

'You know, Molly,' April said, sighing, 'I think I might just do that.'

I almost nearly choked.

Minutes later April was smiling for the first time in weeks. 'It turns out he couldn't sleep either,' she said, coming off the phone. 'He's coming round right now.'

This at least had the helpful result of getting Mum to snap to her senses and realize that she looked like a monster from the Living Dead. 'Oh my goodness, I'd better have a shower and get dressed!' she cried, leaping up the stairs two at a time.

So that is how Nick ended up round at our house with a huge box of chocolates as well as his Important Vet Bag. I wondered where he would have got such a big box of chocolates at such an early time in the morning, but then I

thought, if I was a grown-up who lived on my own, I would probably have huge boxes of chocolates On The Go all the time, so he must have just got it out of the larder.

Nick's eyes went so gooey when he saw April that I thought I would really be sick on the very spot in front of them, so when Frank arrived I was very relieved that he and Molly and I could 'leave the Love Birds to it', as Mum would say.

'Let's have a look at Honey's den,' Frank said.

Aha! I thought. You think that Molly and I are useless girls and that we will not have been able to sort out a den without your manly help. 'Prepare to be amazed!' I said, pushing open the door to the back room to find . . .

'HONEY!'

201

I thought I was supposed to have peace and quiet?

'Is she . . . ? Is that . . . ?' Molly whispered.

Frank gave a low whistle. 'Blimey – she's got a move on,' he said.

Honey – had – had – a – PUPPY!

While we had been making phone calls and worrying about love lives and waiting for Frank to turn up, Honey had quietly given birth.

'I KNEW that was her panting earlier!' I said to Molly a bit accusingly. '*You* said she was snoring!'

'Well, it sounded like snoring,' Molly protested.

'Er, I hate to break up the fight and everything,' Frank said, for once being quite sensible, 'but don't you think we should get your mum or Nick – or both of them? Honey might have another one any minute.'

How to Go Doolally with Excitement

Frank was right. I had read in Monica
Sitstill's book that:

> There are no rules for how much time there is
> In between puppies. I have seen some dogs
> whelp every ten minutes and some have a
> puppy every twenty-four hours.

Soon the house was like a beehive full of active
bees. We were all talking at once. Mum was
boiling the kettle over and over again so much
that I did think for a split of a moment that we
might end up with no electricity left and that
could be quite astronomically treacherous, as
then Nick would not have any light left to see
by if the last puppies were born in the middle
of the night.

While Mum was boiling the kettle into
oblivionation and Molly was jumping up and
down and Frank was pretending that he was
grown-up and checking off things from the

checklist, Nick reappeared from his Quality Time with April, eating Quality Streets, and said:

'You're going to have to ask everyone to calm down, Summer.' Now that he'd seen Honey, he'd obviously clicked out of Gooey-eyed Boyfriend Mode and into Professional Vet Mode. He was rummaging through his big bag and getting out his rubber gloves and his telescope-thingie for listening to Honey's breathing and he was asking me to fetch all kinds of things.

Honey meanwhile was the calmest of all of us, and was gently licking her new teeny-weeny baby and nuzzling it.

 I'm so proud!

'We'd better get ready,' Nick said. 'She may have another at any minute.'

How to Go Doolally with Excitement

'I know,' I said. 'But can't I just have a peek at this one?'

I was desperate to hold it, but Nick said that it was important that Honey wash the puppy and cuddle it before we did.

'If we touch the little one straight away, then it'll have our smell and Honey might reject it. It's really essential that Honey bonds with her babies the minute they are born. Watch – very soon the puppy will start suckling. It's amazing how fast they get to work.'

'Wow! It's just like what it says in my book,' I said. 'They really *do* know what to do by Natural Instinct!'

I was desperate to get Mum and Molly and Frank in the room to see the other puppies being born, but Nick said that we shouldn't have too many people there at the same time. 'It's quite chaotic out there – we don't want

 205

that level of noise and excitement around
Honey. She might get agitated, and that
wouldn't be good for her or the pups.'

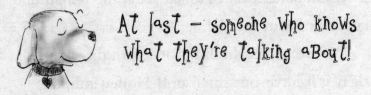

At last – someone who knows
what they're talking about!

So one person was allowed in at a time.

Mum was really keen to get in there, I
knew, but she very kindly said that Molly or
Frank could go first. Frank was surprisingly
gentleman-like about it and said Molly could
go first, which was a good thing as I could tell
by the expression on Molly's face that she was
definitely not prepared to be at all ladylike.

'It's all right,' said Frank, grinning. 'After
all, I have already seen a litter of pups being
born. I was there for all of Meatball's, so it's
only fair that you go before me.'

Molly narrowed her eyes and took a deep

breath and I wondered if she was going to come out with some cutting remark about 'OOOOOOOH! You're such a know-it-all boy, Frank Gritter,' but she just grabbed the opportunity to go and see Honey instead.

Honey had one puppy while Molly was in with her, and then nothing happened for hours and hours and hours. We all hung around the kitchen, dozing off in the chairs with our heads on the table, or trying to stay awake by eating

lots of mince pies and snacks that Mum had bought for Christmas Day.

Every so often, Nick would go into Honey's den to check her heart rate and blood pressure.

'It's OK, she's doing fine,' he kept reassuring us. 'It's quite normal for there to be big gaps like this. I'm not going anywhere – I'll keep checking on her. If there is a problem of any kind I can't deal with here, then I'll whisk her off to the surgery.'

Boy, was I pleased Nick was there.

And it seemed I was not the only one . . .

'Thanks for coming, Nick,' April said, giving him a kiss on the cheek. Nick blushed. Normally I would have felt churningly sick seeing my sister kiss anyone, but bizarrely, I actually felt a WARM AND HAPPY FEELING flutter in my tummy.

How to Go Doolally with Excitement

'Nothing could keep me away,' he said, gazing into my sister's eyes, and I thought perhaps he wasn't talking about Honey's puppies.

In the end we all started talking about sleeping arrangements, as it was pretty obviously going to turn into a night of waiting.

'Mum said I could stay,' grinned Molly, putting down the phone. 'She said, "Think of it as one of your Christmas presents." Do you think that was a cryptical way of saying that at the end of all this I might be able to have one of the puppies?'

I secretly thought that it probably definitely was not, but I didn't want to upset Molly so I just said, 'Mmmm!' and then quickly turned to Frank.

'What about you, Frank?' I asked. 'You should stay too.'

Frank shuffled his feet and muttered, 'Awright. I'll call Mum.'

Mrs Gritter was totally mega-cool about it. She spoke to Mum for a bit and told her, 'It's so exciting – it makes me feel quite tearful to think of one of Meatball's babies becoming a mum! Call me in the morning, won't you?'

'This certainly will be a Christmas to remember,' Mum said as she put the phone down.

She was right about that in more ways than one.

210

16
How to Have an Alternative Christmas

It was the strangest night of my whole life ever. I had been on sleepovers before where we had tried our hardest to stay up all of the night by chatting non-stop. But Mum had always ruined it by coming in every five minutes and saying things like 'I am not going to ask you again –' (this was a load of rubbish, as she always DID ask us again – and again, and again . . .) '– will you please SHUT UP! Some of us have work in the morning . . .' (also untrue, as we mostly had sleepovers at the weekend and Mum did not work at the weekend). Actually, it was not always Mum's fault that we did not stay up all night. Even when we tried our hardest by singing the words to our favourite songs really quietly so that Mum couldn't hear, or by talking non-stop or by having our torches on underneath the duvet, our eyes had this annoying habit of closing and then, before we knew it, we were asleep. (Which is sort of obvious – if you *knew* you were asleep, you wouldn't actually *be* asleep, would you?)

I had said to Mum, 'There is no way that I will *need* to sing a song to keep me awake on the night Honey's puppies are born.'

But even though it really was the most exciting few hours of my life, my eyes were actually beginning to close a bit while Molly was having another turn in the whelping room.

I was sitting in *my* Den (i.e. the non-

playroom) on my favourite beanbag listening to Frank, who was telling me again all about what it was like when Honey was born. I was trying very hard to concentrate, but **weird** things kept happening to my brain.

Frank was saying, 'And then, you just wouldn't believe it, two came out almost at once! Poor Meatball, she was a bit confused. One minute she had one little puppy to lick and cuddle and then there were four . . .'

And I thought to myself, 'I'll just close my eyes for a couple of seconds while Frank tells me about this so that I can picture it in my head . . .' and the next thing I knew, my brain was sending me pictures of Meatball having one hundred puppies at once that had grown wings on their backs and were floating around the den. And Meatball, who had suddenly acquired the gift of human speech, was shouting up at them to, 'Jolly well come

213

back down this instant and do as
you're told.'

But the puppies just ignored
her and laughed and shouted:

'Summer! Summer!'

'Wha-a?' I sat up and shook
my head, which felt a bit blurry.
'What's going on?'

'You were nodding off again,' said

Frank.

'No, I wasn't!' I said crossly.

Frank was laughing at me.

'Yes, you were! And you
were dribbling too.'

I huffed. 'I do not dribble,'
I said, but I quickly wiped
my sleeve across my face just
in case.

'OK,' said Frank, in
his annoying teasing

voice, 'if you weren't asleep just then, what was I talking about?'

'Meatball's puppies,' I said, not mentioning the flying bit.

'Oh, right,' said Frank.

Ha! Sussed him out . . .

'Anyway, don't nod off again,

will you? Nick just came out and said that Honey's had two more pups and he thinks she's only got one to go and then she's done.'

'WHAT?!' I shrieked.

'TWO more! You could have told me! Don't let me go to sleep again, whatever you do!'

Frank grinned.

'So what have you two been up to while I've been with Honey?' Molly had

reappeared and was looking at me and
Frank in a sneery way that made me feel
uncomfortable and anxious.

'What do you mean?' I asked quizzically.

'Look, Summer – when are you going
to admit that Frank's your boyfriend?' Molly
asked impatiently.

Frank's face went such a deep red that I
thought he'd forgotten to breathe. He rushed
out of the room muttering something about
needing a glass of water.

I was so embarrassed and angry about
what Molly had just said that I couldn't speak.

'OK, Summer – I think we're gearing up
for the last pup. Summer? Are you all right?' It
was Nick.

'Ye-es,' I said, avoiding Molly and
following Nick back into Honey's den.

'Do you want to come too, Molly?' Nick
asked.

'No, she doesn't,' I hissed.

Mum took one look at me and Molly and said, 'I think it's time you got some sleep, anyway, Molly. Go up to Summer's room – I've put a fresh duvet cover on. We'll see you in the morning.'

I sat with Nick while my beautiful pooch produced her seventh and final gorgeous baby. I was so tired my teeth were aching, but I would not have missed this for anything. Even the thought of what Molly had just said could not stop the Welling-Up feeling of love and proudness I felt for my beautiful Honey.

Nick went to tell everyone that the last puppy had been born. I think he knew that I wanted a Special Moment all alone with Honey and her new family. It was a Special Moment that went into the CATEGORY of Moments Never to be Forgotten.

I counted: one, two, three, four, five, six . . .

217

Puppy Power

'Seven little soft and squidgy puppies! No wonder you're tired, Honey. Well done, girl,' I whispered, as I bent down to stroke her head.

Aren't they adorable?

There were six golden ones and one black one, and all of them were nuzzled into Honey's side. One of them was making little grunty noises, as if it was snoring. They were silky soft and the cutest teeny-tiny animals I had ever seen! I had not met Honey until she was about two weeks old, and by that time she had grown quite a bit, even though she had still had her eyes tight

shut. Puppies cannot open their eyes straight away. They are actually born blind. It is a miracle to me that they know where their mum is and how to get any milk if they cannot see, but this is yet another thing that they can do just by Natural Instinct.

I was so busy cooing over the pups and whispering to them that I didn't hear Mum and Frank come in.

'Summer, I . . . er . . . think we ought to go to bed.' It was Mum, speaking in urgent and hissing tones in my right ear.

'No way, Mum!' I protested. 'I've waited nine weeks for this mo – ment . . . oh,' I said, as I looked up at Mum and caught sight of something FREAKSOME in the kitchen.

April and Nick were staring deeply into each other's eyes and looked as if they might have a full-on snogging contest right there and then.

219

'Holy Shmoly!' I said in a Molly-type way.

'I'm outta here!' said Frank.

And so was I.

Peace at last.

17
How to Be Exhaustified

The next few days were probably the most hectic of my life.

You think YOU were tired! What about me?

At least Nick was there to help – when he wasn't with April on the sofa, snogging and talking to her in an excruciatingly mortifiable Lovey-dovey manner and generally being yeucksome.

Of course it was brilliant that my sister no longer looked like the Creature from the Black Lagoon, and that Mum was no longer worried about how to Solve the Problem of April's Love Life. However, it would have been better if April didn't take up so much of Nick's Attention Span, as the puppies were basically Running us all Ragged – in other words, we were exhaustified.

For the first ten days, all the puppies did was eat (or rather, suckle) and sleep. The only problem was that they needed more than what I would consider to be a normal amount of food. They didn't just have a sensible number of meals a day, like two or three. Oh no. They

How to Be Exhaustified

wanted their food about sixty million times a day. At least, that's what it felt like.

Food, glorious food!

Normally Honey would have done all of the feeding and not needed a helping hand, as Nature told her what to do. But unfortunately there was a tiny problem with Puppy Number Seven, who quickly became known as Titch. Titch, as you can probably guess from his nickname, was a teeny-weeny thing. He was the Runt Of The Litter, which means that he was the smallest and the weakest. He was born last, and by the time he came out of Honey's tummy, the other puppies had got stuck in and found a place on Honey to feed and get their milk supply. This meant that poor little Titch did not Get A Look In, which basically means he couldn't get any food – in other words, he was in danger of starving.

'This is a common problem, Summer,' Nick had told me. He had tried to encourage Honey to take an interest in Titch, but she was having none of it.

I just want to snooze, you know.

By the next morning Mum had agreed with Nick that we should try to bottle-feed Titch. Luckily Molly and I had been clever enough to Plan Ahead and buy some special puppy milk called 'formula', as it had been on the list that Frank had helped us with.

How to Be Exhaustified

'Can I have a go first?' Molly had asked.

'NO, me!' I had cried. I was still a tiny bit annoyed with Molly for her comment about me and Frank being actual boyfriend and girlfriend, even though she had not mentioned it again since Titch had been born.

Mum had rubbed her eyes and said, 'It's not a game, you two. We have to do this sensibly. And Nick says it's a real commitment, as the puppy has to be fed every two hours to start with.'

EVERY TWO HOURS!

'And this includes through the night,' Mum went on, rubbing her eyes again. 'Nick's going to get some more of that formula milk and some bottles, and then we'll all have to take it in turns.'

So this is why we were all On Our Knees by Boxing Day, which does not mean that we went around everywhere crawling like babies.

225

It means that we were exhaustified from not having slept hardly at all.

We were all so whackeroonied that Mum, April, Nick and I all had to have huge afternoon snoozes. It must have looked very funny – Honey slumped in the whelping box with seven pups snuggled into her, all snoring away, and Mum, April, Nick and I dozing in the armchairs and sofa. If anyone had come round to visit, they would have thought they'd walked into Sleeping Beauty's castle. Except that there were no rose bushes covered in thorns, only a rather droopy-looking Christmas tree and the decorations Molly and I had done. We didn't even have turkey to eat, as Mum

226

did not have time to cook a big meal, what with bottle-feeding Titch and clearing up wet whelping-box paper and feeding Honey and generally keeping track of the pups. We ate turkey pizzas, which were quite gross, and I didn't even open my presents until the end of the day.

When the puppies were about ten days old, things got a little easier for us as we didn't have to feed Titch so frequently. Poor old Honey on the other hand found that life got quite a bit harder because the puppies got pretty active once their eyes started to open. Watching their eyes open was about the most amazing thing I have ever seen. It reminded me of those wildlife films when the camera has been speeded up so that, for example, a flower can be seen blossoming out of its bud in about ten seconds instead of ten weeks or however long it normally takes a flower to un-bud itself. The puppies were like little dog-buds to start with — all curled up on themselves with scrunched-up faces and tucked-in toes. But then they started to sort of straighten out and their eyelids kind of unglued themselves like two bits of sticky paper coming apart very slowly.

Up until this point the puppies didn't seem to realize that we humans existed. We would go into the back room where the whelping box was and clatter around, clearing things up and feeding Honey and so on, and the puppies would keep on snoozing or feeding and would completely ignore us.

I've Brought them up well.

But on the tenth day I went in very early in the morning when it was still dark, and something AMAZING happened.

How to Be Exhaustified

I went to turn on the light, and three of the puppies (including the black one) turned their heads towards me in a scrunchy, blinky way, and then squeaked and scuttled to the corner of their box, all huddled together.

Who's that scary giant?

I had frightened them! I felt rather bad about that, but also quite OVER THE TOP OF THE MOON with excitement, because they had REACTED to me coming into the room! The little black one actually even made a funny little snarly sound! It was possibly supposed to be a scary growl to put me off going too close, but it just made me giggle and feel a bit teary. Those tiny puppies were growing at such a huge and vast rate of speed.

After that morning the puppies became

more and more aware of their surroundings.
And they started to be really quite funny.

Look at us! We can Bounce, We can grow], We can fall over!

'These little guys are just the biggest time-wasters!' Mum said to me one day, when we were still in our PJs at eleven o'clock in the morning.

'What do you mean?' I was sitting on the kitchen floor with all seven pups crawling all over my legs and falling over themselves and each other like little fluffy circus clowns.

'Just look at us!' Mum squealed, plonking herself down next to me. 'All we do is play with the little monsters and cuddle them and swoon over them. I haven't done any proper cooking for nearly two weeks, and the ironing pile is threatening to walk out and find a

woman who actually knows how to plug in an iron and use it.'

Well, that would solve all our problems, I thought.

'You know, it reminds me of when you and April were babies and all I wanted to do was just stare at you all day long,' she said dreamily.

'MUM!' I wailed. 'For the thousand millionth time, will you PLEASE stop comparing me and April to the puppies! It's SOOOO embarrassing!'

Mum smiled at me. 'I can't help it,' she said.

Just then one of the puppies (who was getting distinctly tubbier than his brothers and sisters, I noticed) stumbled into two sleeping pups and jumped back in alarm, yelping. It was so funny and cute!

 Hey, get outta my way, sisters.

'Oh, Mum, look!' I cried. 'Little Tubster looks so shocked!'

Mum giggled. 'Well, the poor love's only just opened his eyes. He probably thought it was just him and the Milk Machine over there until he actually saw his siblings,' she said.

Honey raised her head sleepily and gave Mum a quite dirty look.

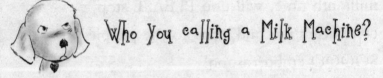 Who You calling a Milk Machine?

Week Three brought a whole load more excitement – the puppies started to bark and wag their tails like proper grown-up dogs! Except that they were still all so mini, that it was like watching Molly's Puppy Power game come alive! Loads of tiny yappy, waggy puppies crashing around and making SO MUCH NOISE! It was FABERooNY.

How to Be Exhaustified

Molly and Frank were at our house practically every second of every day, of course. They had both got vastly interactive where the bottle-feeding was concerned, and Molly was showing particular attention to one little guy.

That would be me — I'm a cutie!

'I am Stepping Up The Pressure at home,' she announced one afternoon.

'What?' I said, a bit puzzled.

'I am trying to be Persuasive and Persistent, just like you were, about having a puppy of my very own,' Molly explained. 'I have set out a list of Pros and Cons and I have made sure that the Pros are definitely winning against the Cons in an amazingly out-weighing manner.'

'What sort of things are in the Pros list?' I wanted to know.

233

Molly got her newest and shiniest notepad from out of her pink-and-purple flower bag. It was a Notebook of Beauty, I had to admit — in other words, I wished I had one like it. It had a soft kind of leathery cover that was actually real golden fabric and it had orange-and-pink stitching on it in the pattern of a flower. It had a little kind of tube of material sewn into the back of the cover and this was where you kept a pen that matched the book. The pages were very light flimsy-type paper like you get in old important books like Bibles or dictionaries, and the edges were golden.

Even Frank said, 'Wow — awesome notebook.'

Molly grudgingly muttered to me that Frank must be OK if he Appreciated her Taste In Stationery. She turned very carefully to a section that was marked with a golden ribbon and began to read.

Pros of having a puppy from the delightful Honey:

---

1) Honey is a mega-lovely dog, so her puppies are bound to be mega-lovely too.

2) Honey has been a wonderful companion to Summer, so one of her puppies would make a lovely companion to me.

3) Summer is not allowed to keep a puppy, so if I did she could come and see it and Honey on a Regular Basis.

4) Having a dog teaches you Responsibilities.

5) Having a dog gets you Out so that you are not always wasting time watching telly and doing Computer-Based Activities.

'But you like watching telly and doing Computer-Based Activities,' I protested. 'Your mum knows that, so she's not going to fall for that, is she?'

Molly winked at me in a know-it-all fashion. 'Aha! I have made a CONSCIOUS effort (in other words, a huge one) to stop playing Puppy Power so much since Honey had her babies, and I have made sure that Mum has noticed this fact. She has even already commented that it is good to see that I am Showing An Interest in something that does not Have A Screen. Also,' Molly continued, 'I have dropped lots of SUBTLE hints about how good for me it would be to have a dog to walk and train in the highly professional manner that you trained Honey. I have been very careful and not Nagging at all – you would be proud of me.' she said.

I had to admit I was quite impressed with Molly's crafty persuasiveness.

How to Be Exhaustified

'But what are the Cons?' I asked.

'Aha! This is the really clever bit,' Molly said, and cleared her throat.

Cons of having a puppy from the delightful Honey:

1) I would have to get up early to let it out and feed it.

2) I would have to go for a walk every day as it is very important that dogs get regular exercise.

3) I would have to be patient so that I could train it properly.

I frowned in bafflement.

'Don't you see?' said Molly. 'I have worded them all so that it says that *I* will be dealing with any potential problems. This is so that

Mum realizes that I am one hundred and ten per cent up for being a responsible dog-owner-type person like you, and she will in the end think this is good for me, and so she will say yes.'

'Hmm,' I said, not particularly convinced. While I was glad that Molly was feeling so positive about her Masterly Plan . . .

. . . I, personally, was not.

But who could resist us?

18
How to Get Emotional

alfway through Week Two, the most treacherously tragic thing occurred: Molly, Frank and I had to go back to school.

'It's sooooo unfair!' I wailed. 'Just as the pups are getting really interesting and actually quite EDUCATIONAL, you are making me go and leave them for hours at a time to learn about useless things such as how to multiply by twelve and who invented the aeroplane!'

'Look at it this way,' Mum said. 'You'll be able to spread the word about the puppies and ask your friends if there is anyone who wants to have one.'

3 x 12 = 36
6 x 12 = ~~72~~

239

Molly crossed her arms and grumped and harrumphed. 'Well good luck to them persuading their parents, is all I can say,' she muttered.

Poor Molly had still not managed to Win Her Parents Round.

I went to say goodbye to Honey and the pups. 'I'll miss you all so much today!' I said, giving them all a hug before I had to get the bus. 'Oh Titch, I'm going to be so sad when you've all gone to your new homes,' I whispered, stroking little Titch's baby-soft fur. 'I can't believe that your mum, Honey, was once as soft and tiny as you. Look at her now . . .'

 What EXACTLY are you saying about me?

On the bus on the way home I asked Molly and Frank how they thought I should Advertise

How to Get Emotional

for new owners. 'Mum says people can come and look at them next week. I know she will start going on at me if I don't have some interested customers,' I said gloomily.

'I think you should do an announcement like I did,' Frank said. 'Remember? "A Puppy is for Life, Not Just for Christmas."'

'Yes,' said Molly, giving him one of her WITHERING looks, 'but that announcement didn't make sense then and it doesn't make sense now. We have just HAD Christmas, so no one is going to get a puppy as a Christmas present, are they—?'

'*Girls* . . .' said Frank cuttingly. 'You're always so picky.'

'Well, BOYS are always so—'

'Guys, I think we're Losing The Plot a bit,' I said, gently interrupting in a DIPLOMATIC way, which means I didn't shout or be rude – in other words, I was tactful and polite. 'We

241

are supposed to be planning how to advertise Honey's pups.'

Molly sighed. 'Maybe I don't want to,' she said.

'Eh?' Frank and I said together.

'Listen, I am DESPERATE for one of Honey's puppies, and I STILL haven't persuaded Mum and Dad. What if we advertise the pups and everyone comes round in one go and there are none left by the morning? It would be a catastrophe of GARGANTUAN proportions,' Molly said. Her eyes had gone a bit watery and I panicked in case they were actually going to start leaking. My poor Bestest Friend. I had not realized how desperate she was.

Frank and I stared gloomily at the floor of the bus. Then Frank suddenly leaped up and almost nearly banged his head on the bag rack. 'I've had the most brilliant idea!' he yelled.

'Did it make your tiny brain hurt?' Molly
muttered.

Luckily I don't think Frank heard her.
'Listen to this: we will only advertise SIX of the
seven puppies – that way there will definitely
be one for you to keep! AND on top of that
ultimately fantastic brainwave, I have had
another one!'

243

Puppy Power

'Careful,' said Molly.

Frank sat down with a bump and said, 'Let's make up a list of Dos and Don'ts for looking after the pups. Then people will know that they must be responsible owners and they won't just rush into asking for one. That will give you more time to work on your mum and dad, Molly.'

Molly raised her eyebrows, pulled the corners of her mouth down and nodded her head slowly. 'Pretty impressive, Frank Gritter. For a boy.'

'Hey, you two! Stop arguing! Anyway, it's our stop – do you want to come to my place and see how the pups have been today?'

'Does Popeye like spinach?' shouted Molly, pushing Frank out of the way in her Haste and Impatience to get off the bus.

We ran to my house and I was in such a palaver of a tizz of excitement that I dropped

244

my front-door keys about a million
times.

'Oh for heaven's sake, Summer!'
Molly cried, and Launched herself at
the doorbell. 'Your mum's here, remember?'

Mum looked a bit FRAZZLED when
she answered the door. 'Thank goodness you're
home!' she said. 'I'm going for a lie-down.'

Anyone would think MUM had given birth
to seven puppies, I thought, but I didn't Dwell
on it, as I was too keen and desperate to see
the little guys.

Molly, Frank and I grabbed some juice and
crept into Honey's den. Poor Honey was flat
out on her side, snoring for England.

I was not. I just had my
eyes closed for a minute.

We sat down quietly and each took a puppy

in our lap. Molly took Titch and stroked him gently.

'You've done so well, little Titch!' she said in a crooning voice. 'Look at what a big boy you are now!'

'Yes,' I said. 'No more bottles for you from now on.'

Once the pups were three weeks old Nick said he would come round to show us how to wean them. We had to encourage them slowly and gently to stop taking all their food from Honey and to start eating some solid puppy food from the shops.

I told Molly and Frank this one night when they were round at mine and read to them what Monica Sitstill's very good advice was about 'How to Wean a Puppy':

'By the start of the third week the puppies begin to explore beyond the whelping box. At this point the pups will need help from you in weaning and house-training.'

How to Get Emotional

'Hmm,' I said. 'I'm not looking forward to that last bit.'

Molly agreed. 'I have very clear memories of how difficult it was to get *Honey* to stop peeing on the floor every five minutes.'

Please don't remind me – it's embarrassing.

Frank laughed. 'You wait! Having seven little ones peeing and pooping everywhere is a Whole Different Ball Game.'

I rolled my eyes. 'What on earth are you on about, Frank Gritter? We are not going to be playing ball games with them. They are too small!'

Frank rolled his eyes back at me and said, 'Oh, shut up and read the next bit!'

I humphed, and stuck my nose back into the book:

'Owners may notice the mother standing up to feed rather than sitting down. This is a sign that she feels the puppies are ready to be weaned.'

The book went on to say that by the end of the sixth week the puppies would be eating puppy food on their own and not drinking Honey's milk any more. I was glad Nick was around to help. I wasn't sure I could manage the weaning thing without him.

Nick came after tea that night when Molly and Frank had gone home.

'Do you want to have a go at feeding the pups by hand?' he asked.

I nodded. There was an excited feeling mixed up with a nervous one bouncing around inside me. I had read all about why we had to feed them by hand. *Perfect Puppies* said that in the wild pups are introduced to raw food when they are still very tiny. Because they don't

always have many teeth at this stage, their mother chews the food for them and then spits it out! Gross! Luckily we didn't have to do that because we had bought special puppy food, I'm happy to say.

The other reason we had to feed the pups by hand was so they realized we were the boss, according to Monica Sitstill.

Nick put some puppy food into a small bowl. 'Ready?' he asked me.

I nodded again and gulped.

April came in to see what we were doing. 'Oh! Can I help?' she asked.

Nick smiled and said, 'Let's take one each. Watch me first.' He bent down and picked up the tiny black boy pup and spoke to it quietly and reassuringly. Then he sat down very gently and put the puppy on his lap. 'It's very important we don't frighten him,' Nick explained. 'We want him to have a good first experience so that he learns to enjoy the puppy food.'

Nick kept on stroking the little black puppy and talking to him quietly, and then with his free hand he reached into the small bowl and scooped up a tiny bit of the food with his thumb and fingertips. He held it under the pup's nose to start with.

'I'm giving him a chance to have a smell first,' Nick explained.

How to Get Emotional

The little guy smelt it for a moment or two and then dug in straight away!

'Hey, he likes it!' I said. 'But won't he bite you? He's getting a bit carried away!'

'If you're quiet and you don't pull away suddenly, you'll be OK. Do you want a go?' Nick asked.

April and I each picked up a puppy and fed them. It was such a great feeling! We stroked them softly and praised them when they'd finished.

Honey had seven very happy little babies that evening. They wagged their tiny tails and rolled around with each other, full of energy from their first meal – and then, just as suddenly as they'd started playing, they fell on each other in a heap and were fast asleep.

Honey looked very proud as she snuggled up with her little babies.

251

We are family! All my sons and daughters with me!

I should have felt so happy and proud that night. After all, I had helped with the Weaning Process and it had been great fun. But somehow I slunk off to bed feeling very low. It was that picture of Honey curled up so happily with her pups that did it.

I didn't want them to go.

19
How to Have the Best of Both Worlds

The next week people started responding to an advertisement that Frank, Molly and I had pinned up on the school noticeboard.

Including Rosie Chubb. Typical.

'Mum says I can have a puppy,' she said, in her usual SpoILT BRAT manner of speaking.

'Does she?' said Frank sarcastically.

'What's it to you, Stinko?' Rosie retorted.

This is a good start, I thought, sighing in my head. I took a deep breath. 'If you have

253

Parental Consent,' I said to Rosie, 'you can come round tonight.'

'WHAAA—?' Molly gasped.

I dug her firmly in the ribs to shut her up. Rosie grinned and pirouetted off like the dancing hippo-ballerina that she is.

'What did you say that for?' Molly hissed. 'You cannot be serious about letting one of Honey's puppies go to live in a house with an overgrown elephant child whose idea of fun is to pick her nose and flick it at anything that moves!'

'Sounds like a great way to pass the day, if you ask me!' Frank grinned, obviously thinking he was De-Fusing the Tension.

'I didn't ask you, Frank Gritter—' Molly spat.

'GUYS!' I shouted. 'I have got to find homes for the puppies. Mum said. So will

254

you please shut up!' and then I ran off to the cloakrooms to hide because I knew I was going to cry. I didn't care if the Queen of England wanted one of Honey's pups. No one would be a good enough owner, as far as I was concerned.

At the end of school I ran out at top speed, avoiding Frank and Molly. I needed to be on my own. I was feeling very Close to the Brim of Tears at the thought of Rosie coming to choose a puppy, and I needed to spend some Special Quality Moments with the puppies.

It was a good job I arrived when I did, as it happened, as April was obviously getting near the end of her tether.

'Am I glad you're here,' she said, puffing out her cheeks and putting her hands on her hips. 'Honey's not cleaning the pups up herself any more – they've started peeing and pooping

255

all over the place! I can't wait to get back to work next week.'

'Oh,' I said.

There was a bucket and a mop out, and soggy newspaper everywhere, and the pups were rolling around and jumping on each other and play-fighting in the middle of all the pALAVER AND MAYHEM. Honey meanwhile was quietly washing herself.

I've done my bit – they're on their own now.

I remembered what it had said in *Perfect Puppies* about toilet training:

256

> To start with, the mother cleans up the pups
> herself. By three weeks, she stops doing this.
> A pup of three to four weeks will urinate twelve
> or more times a day – you can't control this, so
> make sure you have lots of newspaper handy!

I helped April to clear up the soggy newspaper
and told her to go and have a cup of tea while
I laid down some clean sheets of paper.

April came back in once I'd got everything
in order and said, 'Wow, you've done a
great job!' and gave me a hug, which is not
something I think I had ever experienced from
my sister before. It had the Unfortunate Effect
of making me **Brimful of Tears** for the
second time that day.

'What is the matter?' she asked, as I sobbed
into her jumper. 'Have you had a bad day? Is
it Molly? Oh no – is it Frank?'

'NO, IT IS NOT FRANK!' I cried. 'Rosie's
coming round later to choose a puppy and

257

– and – and – I don't wa-ant the pu-pu-ppies
to g-g-g-goooooooo!' I wailed.

April sighed a big WHOoSHY sigh and
said, 'Come on, sit down and have a drink.'
She led me into the kitchen and made me a
hot chocolate.

'How about if I told you something to
cheer you up?' she said as she set the mug of
hot chocolate down in front of me. I noticed as
she did this that she had a new ring on. It was
very sparkLy. I wondered in a vague-ish way
where she had got it from.

'O – K,' I hiccuped. I
went to pick up the mug,
but April was holding
on to it in a limpet-tight
way. 'April, you can let go
of it now, thanks,' I said.

'Haven't you noticed anything?' she
asked, still not letting go of the mug.

258

How to Have the Best of Both Worlds

'Er . . . you've got a new ring on . . . Oh. My. Goodness! YOU'RE ENGAGED?' I shrieked.

April was grinning like that bonkers weirdo cat in *Alice's Adventures in Wonderland*. 'Yes!' she squeaked. 'Nick has asked me to marry him, and I said yes, and we want you and Molly to be bridesmaids. Will you?'

BRIDESMAIDS? Normally I am in no way what could be described as a girly-ish sort of girl, but who in their Right Mind would say no to being a BRIDESMAID?

'DO SWALLOWS FLY SOUTH FOR THE WINTER?' I cried.

April frowned. 'Eh?' she said.

'YES!' I shouted. 'YES, YES, YES, I WILL BE YOUR BRIDESMAID!'

'You've asked her then?' said a voice.

It was Nick, who was also grinning from one ear to the other ear in that **bizzaroid** smiley-cat fashion.

259

April turned round and hugged him, and then they both grabbed me and hugged me too!

Then I remembered about Honey and the fact that her puppies were all about to go to new homes, and I sagged and crumpled.

'I'm very pleased for you,' I said, 'but it still doesn't stop me being sad about Honey's puppies going. What if I never see any of them ever ag-ag-again?' I was getting teary again, and for once I didn't care how babyish it made me look. I felt as though something inside me had snapped open and that I would never ever feel in one piece for the rest of my whole life. Is this what people mean by having a broken heart, I wondered?

April looked quite woebegone and just stood there, as if she did not know what to say or do.

Then Nick coughed and said, 'April?

260

Haven't you told her the other bit of good news?'

'Oh, I'd almost forgotten,' said April, snapping out of her woebegoneness and putting on a huge quite fake-looking smile. I did not think my brain could cope with any more news when my heart was busy falling apart, but April carried on: 'Summer – would it be OK if Nick and I had one of Honey's puppies?'

I didn't know what to be more STUNNED about:

A) my sister asking me something in a polite manner of speaking
B) my sister wanting me and my Bestest Friend to be actual bridesmaids at her real wedding in true life
C) MY SISTER AND HER FIANCÉ WANTING ONE OF HONEY'S PUPPIES!

261

My heart suddenly miraculously repaired itself and I thought instead that my whole body might possibly explode into a million pieces of happiness right there on the very spot. 'You betcha!' I said.

That night, when Mum had also been told all the most exciting news it is possible to be told in one single conversation, she said, 'This calls for a celebration.'

So I phoned Molly and Frank and they came round with their parents, and Nick rushed out for champagne and loads of nibbly things like those crunchy crisps made from parsnips and other disgustingly INEDIBLE grown-up things, and April rushed out after him to buy corn snacks in the shape of aliens and lemonade and other yummily delicious sensible party food.

How to Have the Best of Both Worlds

And when we were all raising our glasses and saying, 'Three Cheers to the Happy Couple!' and laughing and joking and generally having a Whale of a Time, the final, last and most fantabulous thing of all happened.

Mum said, 'Molly and Summer – will you go round and fill everyone's glasses? And Frank, could you pass the snacks around?'

'Sure,' I said. 'But, Molly, where's your mum?' I suddenly asked, as I picked up a bottle and got ready to Do The Rounds.

'She went to find the bathroom,' said Molly's dad. 'Mind you, she's been gone a while – I hope she hasn't got lost. HAR HAR HAR!' He was in quite a *merry* state by then.

Molly glowered at her dad in a very dark way and said, 'I'll go and find her.'

But she didn't need to, because at that moment Mrs Cook appeared, looking quite

263

flushed around the cheeks and smiling in a strange dreamy way.

'Mum!' Molly cried. 'What were you—OH!'

Mrs Cook was holding something in her arms. Something small and soft and snuffly. Something . . . puppy-ish.

'I think we should have this one, don't you?' Mrs Cook said, stroking Titch and looking EXCEEDINGLY pLEADINGLY at Mr Cook. 'That is,' she added hastily, 'if it's OK with you, Summer?'

Molly looked at me and I looked at Molly.

Then Frank said, 'Say something, you loonies!'

And both of us yelled, 'YIPPPPPEEEEEE!'

'What's all the noise?' said a voice.

Oh dear. In all our utter excitement, we had forgotten that Rosie was coming round! She was standing in the doorway with her

264

mum, and the look on her face was one of Feeling Left-outness.

'Sorry,' said Rosie's mum. 'We did ring the bell, but no one heard us, so we tried the door— Oh, you're having a party – would you like us to come another time?'

'No, no!' Mum said, and hurried to find some more glasses.

April quickly filled Rosie and her mum in on all the news, and I interrupted and said, 'There are still five puppies left, Rosie – that is, if you're still interested . . . Do you want to come and see?'

Rosie and I left the others and went into Honey's den.

The pups were all sound asleep.

'It is amazing that they can sleep with all that racket going on next door, isn't it?' I whispered.

Rosie nodded. She was staring at the puppies in TOTAL CAPTIVATION.

265

Puppies have that effect on everyone, I realized, even loud hippo-type annoying girls who are normally rude and OBJECTIONABLE.

'Which one would you like?' I asked.

Rosie just pointed soundlessly at the tiny black boy. 'Can I hold him?' she whispered.

I bent down and scooped him up. 'You'll love this one,' I told her. 'He's just right for you.'

'How do you know?' Rosie asked, but not in her usual sneery sort of way – it was as if she actually wanted to know. I felt quite proud that I knew all about those little poochicals – for me they weren't just little balls of fluff any more.

'He's just not as boisterous as some of the other boy pups,' I explained. 'In Monica itstill's *Perfect Puppies* book it tells you how you can do a personality test to check what kind of TEMPERAMENT your puppy will have — in other words, you can see whether it's going to be quiet or nervous or jumpy or bouncy or shy or whatever,' I said. 'You should get a copy. It's a fab book!'

Rosie carried the little fellow out of the den and went to show her mum.

'Three down, four to go,' I thought. But I didn't feel so sad any more, I realized. These three pups were all going to people I knew and would see quite often. I would not be losing touch with all of Honey's puppies. I would in fact, have the Best of Both Worlds, as I would still be the owner of a totally fantastical pooch myself, and I would be In Touch on a Regular Basis with some of Honey's puppies without having to actually own them.

I went back into the party, feeling quietly happy.

20

How to Have the Happiest of Happy Endings

O ver the next month all the puppies went to new homes. April and Nick took their golden pooch when he was seven weeks old, after Nick had wormed all the pups and had given them their first injections.

'I think we should call this cute little chap "Cupid",' April had said to Nick, 'because if it wasn't for these puppies, we might never have got back together again.'

Mum explained to me that Cupid was the name of an ancient god-type baby with wings had fired his arrows into people's hearts to make them fall in love.

'Urgh. Poor puppy!' I had said.

But as usual April got her way, and so that's what the poor dog was called. I personally thought even 'Meatball' was a better name . . .

 So Do I!

Rosie called her puppy 'Chutney' and had a whale of a time training him. Chutney was the gentlest of the puppies and seemed to adore Rosie ('Each To Their Own' as Molly said.) It was truly a miracle, but for the first time in her life Rosie could be as bossy as she liked to someone and they actually did as they were told!

I'd do anything for my Rosie!

Puppy Power

As for Molly and Titch – they Bonded the minute Molly got him home. Even Mrs Cook admitted to Mum that the palaver of having a puppy was worth it as Molly was doing all the work of looking after Titch and did not 'have her nose stuck in that idiotic puppy game' any more.

She's got real Puppy Power these days!

So all was well that was ending well. April was happy because she had her own dog at last, AND she was marrying the Man Of Her Dreams (yeuck!); Rosie was happy because she had Chutney; Molly was OVER THE TOP OF THE MOON with happiness with Titch, and I was happy because my gorgeous poochical had had gorgeous pupsicles and I would still be seeing at least three of them and losing them for good.

How to Have the Happiest of Happy Endings

Actually there was
one person who wasn't
happy, and that was
Frank. Nick had asked
him to be a pageboy, and Frank had
told me that he would rather 'stick
spiders in his ears and eat drawing pins

for the Duration of the ceremony
than be forced to wear a frilly shirt
and knickerbockers like some kind of
a mental headcase loser-freak.'

'Don't worry, Frank,' I said one day at
school. 'I'm sure we can find a way of telling
Nick Politely But Firmly that you are Not
Interested.'

Puppy Power

But Frank said his mum had told him he had to do it. 'She said it was a great honour,' he moaned. 'What am I going to do?'

Molly thought the whole thing was hilarious. 'You'll look lovely in a gold-and-white outfit with bells round your knees and flowers in your hair!' she teased.

Frank grimaced. 'That's morris dancers, you idiot,' he muttered. 'I don't know why I've been asked anyway,' he continued, turning to me. 'I haven't even known Nick that long, and your sister never spoke to me before the puppies were born. It would make more sense if Honey was a bridesdog.'

'FRANK GRITTER, YOU ARE A GENIUS!' I cried, stopping myself just in time from hugging him.

'What?' he said, in a puzzled and bewildered ~~fashion.~~

~~'Huh?'~~ said Molly, in a Similar Tone.

How to Have the Happiest of Happy Endings

'Molly – you remember when we used
to do our Celebrity Club before we got more
sophisticateder and had our dogs to look
after?' I said, feeling quite out of breath with
excitement at the blinding brainflash
I had just had.

'Ye-es,' said Molly, still looking at me as
if I was the loopiest Fruit Loop in the packet.
'What's this got to do with Frank apparently
taking on Genius Status?' she said sneerily.

'Oh. My. Goodness! This is just too

FANTABULOUS!'

I squeaked. 'Do you
remember in one of
your magazines that
there was a celebrity
wedding with—'
'BRIDESDOGS?'
Molly shrieked,
suddenly clicking

What a GRRReat wedding!
Flanelle dressed her precious
Winnie in pink satin to

took longer to get her bridesdog
dressed than herself. "It's
because I'm worth it," says
Flanelle, three-times winner of
celebrity super-

on to the same length of wave I was on.

'YES!' I shrieked back.

'Holy Shmoly,' said Frank. 'I'm outta here.'

On the bus that afternoon Molly and I decided
we had to tackle the issue of bridesdogs head
on with April and Nick immediately.

'We will need to have a very well-planned
conversation,' I said.

'Yes,' said Molly. 'I think we should
start by paying April loads and loads of
complimentary comments about her choice of
wedding dress and the flowers she is going to
have and so on.'

'And then we'll gently bring the
conversation round to us being bridesmaids
and how we're really looking forward to it,'
I said.

'And we'll just drop in the fact that Frank's
⌐n on the pageboy idea – but we won't

talk about the fact that he would prefer to chew drawing pins,' Molly said.

'No, we definitely won't mention the drawing pins,' I agreed.

'Then we'll show April those really tasteful pictures from my celebrity magazine,' said Molly. 'She can't possibly say no!'

We whizzed round to Molly's and grabbed the magazine. Molly knew exactly where it was, as she had kept all her celebrity magazines in a folder in her desk. 'Just in case they are really valuable one day and I can sell them for lots of money like on that *Roadside Antiques* programme on the telly,' she explained.

Then we grabbed Titch as well, and zoomed over to my place to play with our pooches while we waited for April and Nick to come round after work.

Hi, Mum!

Good to see you, Titch!

The pooches rolled around together in the garden while Molly and I poured over the magazine pictures and planned what outfits we could make for Titch and Honey to make them mega-cute bridesdogs.

'Look at those big velvety bows!' Molly cried, pointing at a floppy dark green bow round one dog's neck.

'That is really classy!' I agreed. 'And look at those leads they've got that are decorated with tiny white flowers – they match the flowers in the bridesmaids' hair!'

'Dudey,' Molly agreed.

'What's that you girls are looking at?' said a voice.

It was April and Nick, here rather early, ...ately.

How to Have the Happiest of Happy Endings

I jumped up in a guilty-ish sort of way and said, 'Nothing!'

But Molly had already picked up the celebrity magazine and was waving the picture of the bridesdogs at Nick and squeaking, 'Look! Look! Bridesdogs!' which had not been in any part of the conversation-planning that we had so far agreed on.

'WHAT?' April shrieked.

Molly stopped waving, and the room filled up with a huge and black kind of silence.

'Bridesdogs,' Molly whispered, as April snatched the magazine from her hand.

My sister glared at the picture on the page.

Just as I thought the world would finally come to an end in a TIRADE of April shouting and screaming at us, Cupid trotted into the kitchen, went right up to April, licked her on the hand and looked up at her with soft, adoring eyes.

I love you!

April's SCARY GLARINESS straight away disappeared. 'How could we even think of getting married without ALL our favourite friends and relations there, darling?' she said to Nick.

So that was how on 26 August, I walked down the aisle behind my sister, carrying a bunch of lilies in one hand and leading Cupid on a leash decorated with daisies with the other. Molly followed with Titch, and Frank dragged his silky-stockinged feet behind us with Meatball on his left and Honey on his right. He'd even washed for the occasion. In fact, he looked a Right Romeo!

'Do you think that might be the end of all your mad and crazy doggy plans for now,

Summer?' Mum teased me at the party afterwards.

'Hmmm,' I mused. 'Maybe for now . . . until Honey has her next litter?'

Mum narrowed her eyes at me. 'OVER MY DEAD BODY, SUMMER HOLLY LOVE!' she growled.

But I did notice she had a glint in her eye . . .